Dedicated to Renèe P.
Most people remember the first book they read, but until I met
your sister, Brianna, I'd never realized everyone also has a last
book they read. It is an honor knowing you chose my Klutz series
to be yours. I didn't get the chance to meet you, but I will always
remember you.

URN MY LOVE

JUST WALK IT OFF
BOOK I

SEDONA ASHE

URN MY LOVE

JUST WALK IT OFF BOOK 1

Sedona Ashe

Cover artwork by Ana Cruz

https://www.anacruz-arts.com

Interior formatting by Cauldron Press

www.cauldronpress.ca

A huge thank you to-

Allison Woerner for Alpha Reading.

Maxine Meyer for Copy Editing.

Imogen Evans for Proofreading & Editing.

Sensitivity Note
(Spoilers Below)

This book has heavy spice as Iolani finds her mates and explores the pleasure their touch gives her. This book mentions one of the mates being held captive and tested on. It also briefly mentions the captors wanting to use him in a breeding program. It also includes a mate who initially doesn't want to accept the fated mate bond; he is cold, not cruel. There are two battle scenes which are violent, and there are multiple deaths throughout this book... *Come on, admit it! Y'all would have been disappointed if I'd left them out!*

CONTENTS

1

IOLANI

"If you could pick up your pace a little instead of stopping to inspect every plant and rock we pass, we'd already be at the lodge and enjoying a cold drink and a relaxing evening."

I couldn't hide my snort.

"What? It's the truth! If I didn't have to escort you, I could've made the journey in half the time." August turned on his horse, pinning me with his moss-green eyes.

Shrugging, I pretended to be unaffected by his attention. "I'm not denying you would already be at the lodge if not for the burden of my presence."

August's eyes narrowed. "Then why the snort?"

Don't say it, Iolani…

I just couldn't help myself. "Since you bring so much joy to every room you exit, I'm finding it hard to believe anyone could find it possible to enjoy an evening in your presence."

August scowled, but not before I caught the twitch at

the corner of his mouth. Despite his best efforts to act as though he despised being stuck with me, he'd nearly laughed and I knew it.

He faced forward again, leaving me to stare at his back... a broad back that tapered to a tight waist. I hated how much I enjoyed watching the muscles beneath his shirt flex as he guided his horse along the trail.

From the moment August had shown up on Ryls' doorstep, I'd been thrown headfirst into one of the most confusing and frustrating experiences of my life—which was saying a lot since it had been less than a month since I was ripped away from the only world I'd ever known and shoved through the veil.

He'd arrived with a small army of gryphons, all eager to greet Trevor. But the instant our eyes locked, August broke away from them and I'd watched him stride toward me. My heart had lodged itself in my throat and my thoughts swirled as I tried to understand the strength of the pull I felt to a complete stranger. And although I was new to how things worked on this side of the veil, I'd known this man was mine.

Having a mate wasn't something I'd considered a possibility until the past few weeks, but now I wondered what it would be like to experience intimacy with a soulmate—or a man, for that matter. And when August had kneeled in front of the swing I was sitting in, and caught my hands between his, I'd never longed for anything more than to experience those firsts with him.

Before I could speak, he'd looked up at me with eyes as

beautiful as an enchanted forest and said, "We will never speak about this to anyone. I'm sure you are a wonderful woman, but I am not taking a mate. Ever."

I'd always prided myself on being an eloquent speaker, a queen who could handle herself in any situation. But finding a soulmate and simultaneously discovering he didn't want a mate was something I hadn't prepared for.

My throat tightened, and all I managed to whisper was a tremulous, "Why?"

The raven-haired man's face twisted in something akin to pain as he stood glaring down at me. "Because I'm not a good man, and I know I can't be a good mate. Not to you, not to anyone. After I offer my congratulations to Trevor, I will sleep for a few hours and then return to the mountains. My presence will never disrupt your life again."

Without giving me time to speak, he walked away, rejoining the gryphons. Summoning the royal facade I'd perfected over the years, but was sick to death of being forced to hide behind, I pulled it around me as though it were my armor—or the comforting embrace of the weighted blanket Ryls had put on my bed. The first night I'd slept under it, I'd thought it was enchanted or possessed and was trying to smother me. But now I enjoyed its reassuring weight as I slept.

I'd claimed to have a headache, and retreated to my room, burying myself under the blanket. My plan was to stay there until the following day, hoping that would give my not-soulmate time to rest, then leave without us bumping into each other.

It hadn't worked out that way, though. I'd barely been in my room for two hours when every muscle in my body spasmed and convulsed before going taut. My skin burned, and I kicked off the blanket to find blue flames licking over my skin. No sooner had they appeared, then they disappeared, leaving my body feeling colder than ice.

Goosebumps spread across my skin, and each ragged breath was visible in the air. Needle-like pain stabbed every inch of my body, as though frostbite was setting in. But how was that possible? Frostbite wasn't really a phoenix type of problem.

Before I could do more than whimper, my vision turned to absolute darkness. No, not completely dark. Something moved in the corner and I struggled to focus on it. Slowly, I cleared away enough of the shadows and blur to look around. It wasn't my room I was seeing; it was a room I didn't recognize.

Lifting my head, I stared out a window that overlooked a sprawling forest that seemed to extend as far as the eyes could see. My body suddenly turned from the window, and I realized with a start it wasn't my body. I was simply a passenger, viewing the world through someone else's eyes.

A pale hand with perfectly manicured, black-tipped fingernails picked up a brochure and flipped it open. The cover read Amber Bluff Lodge and showed a large wooden cabin surrounded by towering trees. Another page showed a sprawling barn and smiling people riding horses down a trail.

Before I could read the back, my head began to ache,

and my vision blurred. The brochure fluttered to the table, landing next to a chessboard with pieces scattered across the board.

With my stomach pitching wildly, I tried to focus, desperate to figure out whose eyes I was viewing the world through. My eyes darted from piece to piece on the chessboard, hoping to find a clue there. It was useless, though. Darkness bled from the edges, and the last thing my eyes landed on was the black knight before I was swallowed up by nothingness.

The return to my body was violent, as though someone was ramming my consciousness back into my body.

"What's wrong? Talk to me!" a deep voice growled.

My eyelids fluttered open, and I looked into the eyes of the last person on earth I wanted to see.

The man who'd made it clear he didn't want me.

I opened my lips to demand an answer, but my stomach churned and sent bile rushing up my throat. Clamping a hand over my mouth, I lurched off the bed, only to discover my trembling legs were too weak to support me.

Toppling forward, I braced for an impact that never came, thanks to the strong arm that looped around my waist. The man easily lifted me into his arms and carried me to the bathroom.

He sat on the floor beside the toilet with a gracefulness I found surprising considering his hulking size, and positioned my quivering body on his lap so I could expel the contents of my stomach. As the room spun, and my muscles continued to quake, the stranger held my hair, murmuring soft sounds of pity.

It was humiliating.

He was seeing me at the lowest point I'd been in since tumbling onto this earth. And although he'd made his stance on mates crystal clear, I hated that I still longed for him. Not for his body, because at that moment the last thing I wanted was sex, but for the intimacy of having a life companion who loved me during the highs and lows.

When I finished emptying my stomach, I sat motionless on his lap, wishing I could pull a Ryls and die. I'd go straight to the afterlife, but unlike Ryls, I'd stay there so I'd never have to face him again.

"Thank you for your help," I whispered, trying to keep my voice from betraying how horribly vulnerable I felt in that moment. "You can go now."

I was the queen of the afterlife. This wasn't a position I was used to being in.

The man gave a low laugh, making no move to leave. He continued cradling me in his arms, gently raking his fingers through my tangled blue hair.

Calling up every scrap of dignity I could muster, I slowly pushed to my feet and staggered to the sink to wash my face and brush my teeth.

The man remained seated on the floor, and although I refused to look at him, I felt his gaze burning my back.

I'd nearly finished when another wave of dizziness swamped me, and my legs buckled. In the blink of an eye, his hands were on my waist, steadying me. I sucked in a breath, stunned that a man built like a grizzly bear could move with the speed of a cheetah... or a striking viper.

Bending forward, I rinsed my mouth and toothbrush, trying to ignore the way my backside pressed against him, or the way the mid-thigh silk gown was riding up. When I straightened, our eyes met, and for several heartbeats, neither of us spoke as we studied each other's reflections.

The man in the mirror seemed somehow less intimidating and cold than the man I'd met outside, and I couldn't stop myself from asking, "What's your name?"

His fingers flexed on my hips, and I didn't think he'd even noticed the way his thumbs were rubbing gentle circles on my gown. He took so long to answer, I thought he'd decided against sharing even that part of himself with me.

"August." His jaw clenched, then he asked, "And yours?"

"Iolani."

In the mirror, one dark eyebrow rose. "That's a Hawaiian name, isn't it? Meaning royal hawk?"

I couldn't hide my shock and twisted around to face him. "How did you know the meaning of my name? I've never met anyone who knew."

"Languages have always fascinated me, and I took an interest in 'Ōlelo Hawai'i a couple of decades ago." His eyes drifted to my lips and darkened.

Was he thinking about kissing me? Did I want him to?

Yes.

No.

Maybe.

If he truly didn't want me, then I didn't want to accept his touch. But I was finding the pull between us hard to resist, and my curiosity over how it would feel to have his lips against mine was overwhelming.

I focused on the one thing that had always helped to ground me. Duty.

Azurea was on earth, and the veil was unstable between our worlds. I had work to do. According to Ryls and her mates, a mate could help me grow stronger so I could fix things before the balance between worlds was damaged forever.

I was willing to give my all to a relationship, but I couldn't sacrifice valuable time on a fling. Even if I was dying of curiosity to know what could feel so good, that Ryls and her mates were apparently willing to give up countless nights of sleep to indulge in it. Earplugs had become my best friend since we'd arrived on earth.

Ignoring the delicious heat arching between our bodies, and how much I wanted to taste his lips, I wiggled out from between his body and the sink. With as much decorum as I could muster, I made my way to the small desk in the room's corner and flipped open the laptop Jett had brought me the first week I'd been on earth.

He'd spent most of the day teaching me how to use it, and while he didn't explicitly say it, I understood it was his way of showing gratitude for helping return Ryls to them—even though it had come with severe consequences for me. I hadn't wanted to bother Ryls while she was resting and spending time with her mates, so being able to binge watch various shows had helped to pass the time. It also helped me familiarize myself with various human customs and learn some slang, so I could attempt to blend in more while on Earth.

I typed the name of the lodge into the search bar and waited impatiently for the results to load.

"Thank you again for your unexpected kindness. I'm feeling much better and have some work to do." Not wanting August to see the sadness I knew had to be lurking in my eyes, I kept my gaze on the webpage and just used my fingers to wave toward the door.

Instead of leaving, his footsteps drew closer until he could lean his hip against the desk. "What happened earlier? I heard you cry out. When you didn't answer my knocking, I came in and found you unresponsive. You were ice cold, but covered in sweat. I'm not a doctor, but that's not normal. Are you sick? Will it happen again?"

Unable to help myself, I snapped, "It might, I don't know. But I'm not your problem and I don't know why you suddenly care what happens to me."

It had come out sharper than I'd intended, and closing my eyes, I tried again. "I've got a lot going on and it's probably just stress. If I feel bad, I'll have Ryls call a doctor."

I knew it wasn't a human illness, but I had no desire to confide anything else in him. He'd been clear he wasn't sticking around, and I'd never see him again once he left. That meant there was no reason to waste time with small talk.

"You were glowing." August made no move to leave.

I found a page that looked promising and clicked the link. "I do that sometimes."

"You aren't going to tell me what you are, are you?"

"There's no need. We aren't mates, nor are we friends. I sincerely appreciate your help during my"—I paused, searching for the right word—"episode. But you've made your decision regarding us, without asking for my input. I respect that, but you should probably leave before someone catches you in here. You don't want us to speak about it again, so I'm guessing you don't want anyone to know. So you should leave before someone catches you in here and gets the wrong idea."

August's breathing was rough, but he remained silent. Ignoring him, I scrolled down the page, reading about the lodge.

It was located in the United States, quite far from the compound, and was in a remote location in the middle of a wilderness accessible only by horseback. I knew Xerxes could get a pilot friend to take me there. He'd already told me he'd provide anything I needed to complete my mission. All I needed to do was say the word.

I'd get a flight to the nearest airport and then take a trail up to the lodge. Having spent countless hours on horseback on Cucalas, I wasn't worried about my ability to ride, even in unfamiliar terrain.

Clicking *print*, I stood and gathered the papers from the tiny printer tray. Walking to the bed, I bent and pulled out the backpack Ryls had ordered for me, and stuffed the papers in the front pocket. I continued to ignore the man who remained still, other than his eyes, which tracked every move I made.

It was odd that I'd only felt sadness at his initial denial of the mate pull between us, but after he'd given me a glimpse in the bathroom of what it would be like to have him as my mate, fury had built in my chest. He'd decided he wasn't worthy to be my mate, without even knowing a single thing about me.

Had he decided I was a delicate woman who'd crumble to pieces the first time he hurt my feelings? To be fair, him finding me mid-vision, or whatever that was, didn't paint me as a strong woman. But that couldn't be further from the truth.

I was the Queen of the Phoenix Afterlife, and I was preparing to fight a battle between worlds. If I failed, the veil could end up collapsing and taking out one, or both, worlds. I was still rebuilding my strength after using everything I had to get Ryls back to the living. Being yanked through behind her, into a world I wasn't used to living in, had taken its toll on me too.

But this weakness was temporary, and I knew I would be at full strength soon. And if Ryls was right, I'd be stronger than ever before if I bound myself to a soulmate. But if this man was going to judge me at my weakest, he didn't deserve me at my best...

Even if he was gorgeous, and every fiber of my body was begging to go to him.

August finally spoke. "Are you going somewhere?"

I pulled a stack of jeans and shirts from the drawer. "Yes. Since I'm leaving, you have no need to rush away. You can stay and visit with Trevor without worrying you'll bump into me."

From the corner of my eye, I caught the jerk of a muscle in his jaw. "Where are you going?"

I moved to the closet and grabbed a pair of hiking boots. They weren't ideal for riding, but they had an okay heel and would do. I quickly packed the basic toiletries and dropped them into the backpack. Opening the nightstand drawer, I grabbed the satellite phone Mace had bought me and stuffed it in the bag. I knew I wouldn't involve Ryls in this battle unless I had to, but I wanted to be able to check in and assure myself she was safe.

All that was left was to change clothes, but August still hadn't moved from where he leaned against the desk. His eyes were scanning the website I'd left up, and I kicked myself for not closing it.

An unfamiliar feeling stirred in my chest, and it took me a moment to figure it out. Spite. If he was willing to pretend his soulmate didn't exist, then I would do the same.

Turning away from him, I slid the thin straps of the gown over my shoulder and let the silk slip down my body to pool on the floor around my feet. Forcing myself to remain unhurried, I grabbed the thick denim jeans and bent to put first one foot and then the other into the legs. They were tight, so it took a bit of wiggling to get them on.

Still acting as though August was invisible, I pulled the tight sports bra over my head. It wasn't the sexiest choice, but anyone who's spent some time on a horse's back knows having the bouncy bits snug was more important than appearance.

Slipping into a short-sleeved shirt, I moved to the mirror to pull my hair up in a ponytail.

Refusing to make eye contact with the man standing in the shadows, I lifted the backpack onto my shoulder and grabbed the jacket off the back of the door, then I headed out of my bedroom to find Xerxes.

It didn't take long, and after leaving a note for Ryls that I had to check something out, but would check in, I headed out the front door. One of Xerxes' men sat in a sleek black car, waiting to take me to the airstrip. Not wanting to risk Ryls coming in from the backyard and trying to go with me, I hurriedly slipped into the backseat.

"Thanks for driving me. Let's go."

He put the car in drive, but before he could let his foot off the brake, the left rear door opened and August slid in beside me.

"What are you doing here?" I demanded, scowling at him.

He leaned back against the seat and looked straight ahead. "I'm coming with you."

No, he absolutely wasn't going with me here or there... he would not be coming with me anywhere.

"I didn't invite you," I snapped, shooting a look at the front door and hoping Ryls wouldn't make an appearance.

She was overly protective of me and wouldn't want me to leave alone, but I refused to risk her or the baby.

"I don't care. Either I come with you, or I will go tell Amaryllis you are ill and trying to sneak off on a strenuous misadventure." August kept his gaze straight ahead, not looking at me as he waited for my decision.

He was blackmailing me, and I wanted to fry his sexy backside for it. The only issue was my powers wouldn't truly harm him if he was a fated mate, or at least that was how it worked for phoenixes born outside of Cucalas.

It was easy to put on an act and pretend my heart wasn't aching for my soulmate for a few minutes. But how was I going to keep up the facade of not caring for hours in his company?

"Why?" When he didn't answer, I told the driver August was going with us and collapsed against the back seat of the car in defeat.

Now, looking at the muscles rippling under his shirt, as he guided his horse up the trail in front of me, I knew I'd been right to worry. Every hour in his company made it harder to convince my heart he didn't belong to me. I'd been able to avoid him on the long plane ride, but now that we were alone on a trail, it was impossible.

Why had he forced his way on this trip? When he'd first met me, he couldn't get away from me fast enough. Now he refused to let me out of his sight.

I'd never been so confused in my life.

2

AUGUST

My thighs hurt, my back hurt, and worst of all, my balls hurt from bouncing in a saddle for hours. It had been years since I'd ridden a horse longer than an hour or two in a single day.

Now I was on a trip that shouldn't have taken more than a day at most, but at the pace Iolani was moving, it was going to take two full days. You'd think she'd never seen rocks or flowers before, by the way she stopped to admire them. Despite my annoyance, the fascination on her face when a new bird called from the forest depths was something incredible to behold.

She was breathtakingly gorgeous, and I hated myself for noticing.

It was a special kind of torture, and I couldn't figure out why I'd pushed myself into her trip. Why had I rushed to her room when I'd heard her cry out? Why had I stayed with her while she was sick?

It was as though she'd pulled me to her like gravity, and now that I was in her orbit, there was no escaping.

But why did it have to be her? I'd known for years I would never take a mate. My heart was too cold, and while I cared for the gryphons, I did it from a sense of duty rather than a sense of love. I wasn't even sure I was capable of love.

I was a great guard for the gryphon pride, because I could kill and sleep like a baby a few minutes later. Inside, I felt nothing. Not happiness, guilt, joy, or sorrow. I'd never even experienced lust, let alone love.

Until her.

It wasn't like a dam had broken and let feelings burst free inside me. No, it was more like a tiny crack had appeared, allowing emotions to trickle through it. But even that was more than I'd experienced before, and I blamed my curiosity for not allowing me to walk away.

Fear wasn't something I was familiar with. It was a trait that made me an excellent killer, since I wasn't distracted by concerns about dying. Yet, when I'd heard her cry, and then rushed into her room to find her sheets soaked with sweat while her body felt as though she'd been submerged in icy waters, my chest had tightened.

It was uncomfortable, and I'd hated it.

When she'd sat on my lap, emptying her guts and shivering, my stomach had twisted with concern. It was not a sensation I enjoyed.

But when her body pressed against mine as she brushed her teeth, and then when she bent over to get the backpack from beneath the bed and her gown had slid up, flashing her perfect butt, I'd experienced an awakening of something I *had* enjoyed.

It had only increased when she'd grown annoyed with my stubbornness to leave the room and changed in front of me. The gown had rippled down her curves before hitting the floor and leaving her in nothing but the blue thong. My erection had strained against my jeans and I'd realized with a shock that she'd made me harder than I'd ever been with nothing more than a flash of her milky skin.

I should've stormed from the room, shifted and taken to the skies to put as much space between us as possible. But I hadn't.

Because as soon as I'd realized she was planning a solo trip into the wilderness, my chest tightened and a thousand ways she could be hurt or killed flashed through my mind.

I'd decided to escort her to the lodge to make sure she got there safely, and reassure myself she wasn't going to have another episode like the one I'd found her in while alone on a trail.

Then I could leave and never look back.

A growl rumbled in my chest, forewarning me that was going to be easier said than done. I might not have a heart or the ability to love a mate the way she deserved to be loved, but I was strong enough to deny myself and give her a chance at finding it with someone else.

The next few hours passed relatively quietly. Iolani thankfully stopped less often, so we covered the distance faster. While we wouldn't make it to the lodge that night, we'd only need to ride a couple of hours in the morning before arriving.

An hour before sundown, we stopped to groom, feed and water the horses. Once they were cared for, I strode into the woods to have a few minutes away from the woman who was causing me to be more unsettled with each hour that passed in her presence. When I returned just after sunset with an armload of wood for a fire, I found her sitting in front of a crackling campfire.

She glanced up at me as she took a bite of her granola bar, neither of us saying a word. Iolani broke the silence by reaching into her backpack and holding out several granola bars for me to take.

I'd bought trail supplies at the stable at the beginning of the trail where we'd borrowed the horses, but I couldn't resist taking what she offered me. Settling on the log across from her, I opened a granola bar, and we ate in companionable silence.

After eating, we unrolled our sleeping bags and settled in under the stars to sleep. It was going great until I woke to the sound of the campfire popping and hissing as large drops of rain began to fall. It was one of the freak rain showers that wasn't uncommon in the area, but it was an annoyance, since we didn't have the protection of a tent.

Iolani was still asleep, but had burrowed deeper in her sleeping bag until just her blue hair spilled out. As the rain fell harder, and the fire went out, I realized our sleeping bags weren't going to keep either of us dry or warm.

I'd camped in worse conditions, but I didn't want to risk

Iolani getting ill. Rising to my feet, I moved soundlessly around the dying fire to where Iolani lay. Stretching myself out beside her, I partially shifted and stretched my large smoke-colored wing over her. It was large enough to cover all of her body and most of mine. Even as the rain fell harder, the water slid down my feathers, leaving the ground beneath my wing dry.

With the mate I could never have tucked under my wing, I felt something I thought might be contentment and fell asleep dreaming of things that could never be.

WAKING THE NEXT MORNING, I lifted a hand to rub the grit from my eyes, only to stop at the brush of feathers against my arm. They were far softer than my coarse, stiff feathers, and I stared in awe.

Iolani had sprouted a pair of silver wings, and beneath the shelter of my much larger wing, she'd snuggled her face against my chest and draped her wing around me in a feathered embrace. Before I could think better of it, I tucked a strand of long blue hair behind her ear.

Iolani murmured something, scooting tighter against me. Knowing how annoyed she was going to be when she woke and realized she was snuggling me had my lips twitching in amusement.

My smile faded as a sudden longing to wake every morning with her in my arms caused my heart to ache. But

I couldn't do that to her just because I enjoyed how she made me feel something.

What I could offer her was nothing more than shadows compared to the love she could get from a better mate. If she needed someone killed or shaken down, I was the man for the job. But cradling her while she cried, or being aware of when she needed emotional support, those were things I didn't understand, so I couldn't offer her.

Shaking off the dark thoughts, I studied the woman in my arms. She was tall, but compared to my six-foot six-inch height, she seemed small and easily broken.

My eyes traveled across her feathered wing. What was she? Some type of bird shifter? Trevor had been tightlipped about what had been going on with his mate. I knew Amaryllis was the last phoenix, so this woman couldn't be a phoenix. If she was a gryphon, I would have smelled it on her, so that couldn't be it either. Her wings were feathered like a bird, so that crossed-out dragon.

I was dying to ask her, wanting to know more about her, but I shoved the questions back. In a matter of hours, I would leave and never see her again, so the less I knew, the better.

Still, I couldn't resist the urge to stroke the back of my finger down one of her feathers. Her wing twitched in response, but Iolani's breathing remained even. Growing more daring, I brushed the back of my hand against her wing, loving how incredibly soft the feathers were against my skin.

I glanced back at her face to find her bright blue eyes

watching me. Since she made no move to stop me, I gave into my urge to stroke her wing again, a flicker of heat coming to life in my stomach when her lips parted and she sucked in a breath.

For gryphons, our wings were extremely sensitive, and I wondered if it was the same for her. Judging by her quickened breathing and the slight tremble of her wing, I was guessing the answer was yes.

"You kept us dry last night." Her voice was husky with sleep.

"Yes," I answered simply.

"Thank you."

The soft, open woman in my arms reminded me of how she'd been the day before, when I'd held her after she was sick. Then she'd built walls between us and had shifted into a woman with a mission. She was strong, and I admired her for it. But I liked this vulnerable side too.

Pulling her arm out from beneath her wing, Iolani reached up to brush the underside of my wing. It was the first time my wing had ever been touched by anyone other than me and I wasn't prepared for the effect it would have on me.

The flickering warmth in my belly spread through my body, and I barely managed to swallow back a groan.

Iolani continued to stroke the length of the feathers she could reach, her fingers tracing along the shimmering black tips. Gryphon plumage came in a variety of colors and patterns. When my wings were closed, they appeared to be a dark gray. Up close, the base of the feathers were such a pale gray they were almost white, which blended into a medium gray before turning almost black at the tip. It was an interesting ombre effect that few other gryphons possessed.

The tip of each of my feathers had a black foil-like appearance that shimmered when it caught the light. In battle, my wings almost appeared to be made of thousands of sharp-tipped blades, a terrifying effect that instilled fear in my enemies' hearts moments before I sent their souls to Hades.

Yet now those powerful wings that had helped me slaughter armies were on the verge of trembling from nothing more than the briefest touch from the blue-haired beauty in my arms.

Not willing to let her see how she affected me, I rolled away from her and stood. Folding my wings against my back, I shifted so that they disappeared and made my way back to my soaked sleeping bag.

"We should get on the trail. The lodge is only about two hours away, and the sooner I can drop you off there, the sooner I can return to my business."

It was a lie. I had nowhere on earth I needed to be. Most of my days were spent guarding the gryphon pride, or taking the odd job that was too messy for the various government militaries to get involved in officially.

I'd been well-compensated over the decades and had spent very little, so I could afford to never work another day for the rest of my very long life. But she didn't need to know that.

Without a word, Iolani had rolled to her feet, and I tried not to notice she'd taken her shirt off to free her wings and now wore nothing but a bra from the waist up.

My pants grew tighter, and with a growl, I pulled my shirt on over my head and moved to saddle the horses.

3

IOLANI

I was getting whiplash from how fast this man could shift from gentle giant to grouchy troll. Last night, when I'd rolled over to find myself tucked under the protection of his wing, my heart had swelled with affection.

Just like when I'd been sick, he showed me a tender side of himself, one that was easy to fall in love with. I wasn't used to being taken care of, because I was the one who protected everyone else.

He'd laid on the ground beside my sleeping bag, with dirt and sticks poking his body as he slept. And since he'd removed his shirt to free his wings, his back had been exposed to the rain and the frigid night air. I gently rested my hand against his chest. His skin was several shades darker than mine, and I paused to admire the beautiful contrast. Beneath my palm, he felt cold, and I'd longed to show him the same consideration toward his comfort as he'd shown toward me.

Careful not to awaken him, I pulled off my shirt and spread my wings. Swallowing hard, I scooted closer to him and wrapped my wing as best I could over his chest and shoulder.

I called for the fiery magic in my chest, using it to raise my temperature until I was the human equivalent of a hot water bottle. In his sleep, August had instinctively hooked his arm over my waist and drew me closer.

At first, my muscles had been stiff with tension, but then I'd given in to the desire to be held for just one night in his arms. Tomorrow he would leave me, but while he slept that night, I could pretend he was mine.

I'd been awakened by his fingers caressing my wing, and I'd been shocked to find it was more intimate than any of the sexual things I'd imagined. When I'd gathered enough courage to stroke his wing, and saw the way his eyes glowed in response to my touch, I'd thought maybe he'd changed his mind.

Maybe he was going to give us a chance.

Then he'd abruptly stood and strode into the woods without so much as a backward glance.

August had claimed he didn't want the bond because he wasn't good enough, but I couldn't help but wonder if it was something about me he didn't like. If I'd been someone different, then would he have loved me?

With a heavy heart, I packed my things and started toward the horses, only to stop when I noticed how soaked his sleeping bag was. Squatting beside it, I ran my hands over the fabric. I sent heat into it, and watched with satisfaction as steam rose, until every last drop of water had evaporated.

When I finished, I headed to my horse and found he'd already been saddled. I looked around for August but couldn't spot him. Chewing my lip, I debated waiting for him to show, but decided I'd go ahead and hit the trail. He liked to move faster than me, so it wouldn't hurt to get ahead of him.

Gently tapping my heels and clicking my tongue, I guided the gorgeous buckskin back onto the trail that wound ever higher toward the lodge.

WE REACHED the lodge faster than expected. Probably because my anxiety was pushing me to hurry, and I'd been too distracted to notice the view as we traveled.

Visions weren't something I'd experienced in Cucalas, and I wasn't sure why I would have one now. I'd spent hours trying to puzzle it out, and my best guess was my link to Azurea was allowing me to catch glimpses of what she was seeing.

While I could always sense her presence, and know when she was near, this felt different. It was as though an invisible thread was pulling me to the lodge. But maybe that had to do with Earth's effect on the link that had been created between us when she'd been marked by my magic during our battle so long ago.

Here I was, rushing toward who knew what, and I hadn't even figured out how I was going to deal with her once I found her. It had taken a lot out of me when I'd beat her the last time, and I wondered how I could do it now while still depleted. I was the queen of the phoenixes, yet Amaryllis was probably stronger than me at that moment.

Shoving aside my concerns, I focused on the feeling in my chest that urged me to hurry.

The lodge seemed deserted when we plodded from the woods into the cleared land surrounding it. Dismounting, I led my horse into the barn beside the lodge. To my relief, a stable hand was inside, busy mucking out a stall.

"If you want to tie up out front, I'll take care of him and you can head into the lodge and get settled in." He gave me a wide, welcoming grin. "Gino told me a pair of riders were making the trek up on horseback from their barn to the lodge, so I've been waiting on y'all. I bet you two are ready to eat and sleep in a real bed."

I returned his smile. "Thank you, but I'd like to help. Hosea was such a gentleman the entire ride, so I want to make him comfortable before I go inside."

"Alrighty. Well, the tack can be hung in the room there" —the man motioned to a small room off to the left—"and the brushes can be found in the baskets there."

He pointed to large wire baskets nailed to the wall that held various grooming tools. "I'll get the stalls ready while you two tend to that."

With a tip of his hat, he strode down the long aisle toward the back of the barn. August appeared at my side, and despite my protests, he removed my saddle. When he finished with mine, he began removing the tack from his handsome horse.

By the time we finished brushing them, the man had returned. Clipping two lead ropes to their halters, he led the two handsome horses away.

The exhaustion from the trip hit me all at once, and I headed for the lodge, ready to find a bed to crash in. Pushing open the heavy hand-carved door, I found the inside of the lodge was just as desolate as the grounds outside.

"Well, howdy, folks."

My eyes darted in the direction of the booming voice. A man with a beard that reached mid-chest and bushy white eyebrows was leaning back in an office chair with his boots kicked up on the reception desk.

He pulled out a pocket watch and glanced down at it. "I figured you'd be here last night. Did you run into trouble on the trail?"

His tone was that of a worried father rather than one of annoyance.

My cheeks warmed. "No, I just found the trail so beautiful and I couldn't keep myself from stopping to admire the flora and fauna."

The man's eyes sparkled. "I'd say that's a pretty good way to enjoy a trip. You know what they say—you gotta take time to stop and smell the roses."

I'd never heard that, but I liked it. "Do you still have room for us?"

The man's eyes darted around the silent, empty lounge area and he raised a single caterpillar-like eyebrow. "With the current crowd, I'll have to check to see if we have some vacancy."

I nodded while trying to figure out if he was being sarcastic or if he was being serious.

"I'm just teasing, little lady." He chuckled and handed me two keys. "Here are the keys to the two rooms. They are adjoining rooms, but you can keep the door locked between them if you prefer."

I stared at the keys, my forehead creasing. "But I haven't paid for the rooms yet."

"Your travel agent took care of that for you yesterday. It was X something." He shuffled a few papers. "Ah! Here it is: Xerxes Drakon. He said you'd be tired after the trip, so he wanted to make sure the paperwork was taken care of so you could rest after arriving."

Surprised, but not exactly shocked, I murmured my thanks and headed down the hall to find my room.

"*The* Xerxes Drakon is your travel agent? He makes the world's criminal underbelly tremble in fear, but calls to make reservations for you?" August's deep rumbling laughter did weird things to my stomach. "For those words to come from his mouth, you either outrank him in power, or Ryls found out he knew you were leaving and didn't stop you, so she demanded he make sure you were okay. I'm guessing it's the latter."

"Hm," I answered noncommittally.

Both were likely true, but I didn't correct August. He

didn't need to know anything more about me. When my work finished here, I wasn't even sure which side of the veil I would be stuck on.

As much as I liked earth, Cucalas needed me, and once I was there, he would never see me again. So why waste any more of my energy on the stubborn, silent man who'd be gone in a few hours?

Finding the first room, I handed August the second keycard and quickly let myself into the room. I closed and locked the door behind me, not giving him a chance to follow me inside.

With the flick of a switch, the lamps in the corners of the room flickered to life, and I experienced a sense of déjà vu.

This was the exact room from my vision, down to the brochure on the small table by the window and the chess-board set up beside it.

Sagging down on the bed, I dropped my backpack to the floor and stared out the window. I didn't sense Azurea's presence here. So now what?

Worse, the urgency in my chest had grown stronger, driving me to follow it… but to where?

I'd come to this lodge in the middle of nowhere, confident I'd find the answers here. It hadn't occurred to me that I should've come up with a backup plan.

Flopping back on the bed, I wiped at the stray tear sliding down my cheek. I hated this. My life had been one of order, one where I knew exactly what was expected of me.

Now I was stumbling around in a world I didn't fully

understand, and without a clear plan. Find enough power to stabilize the veil, trap Azurea back in Cucalas, and then permanently repair the veil between our worlds.

Easy, right?

Not.

And the only person who might've been able to help me on this mission had taken one look at me and decided we'd never work out.

It was fine. I was strong and I could figure something else out. This wouldn't be the first time I'd beaten Azurea, but I was sure it would be the last. I'd never allow her to risk anyone else's safety again.

My eyes drifted closed, and curling into a ball on the bed, I fell into a fitful sleep.

Several hours later, I was awakened by a large hand gently shaking my arm. If it hadn't been for the tingling electricity his touch sent across my skin, I might have been scared. But even with my eyes closed and mind foggy with sleep, I knew August's touch.

"I've brought food. You need to eat dinner."

"How did you get into my room?" Groaning, I pressed my fingers to my eyes and sat up.

He refused to meet my eyes. "The door lock was weak between our rooms."

"So you broke into my room? To feed me? Seriously, you give off more mixed signals than a broken orb."

"A what?" August's eyebrows drew together.

Realizing I'd said too much, I took the spoon and stuffed my mouth full of the stew he'd set in front of me. "This is delicious! What is it?" I shoved another spoonful of the buttery chicken and dough soup into my mouth.

"It's called chicken and dumplings. You've never had it before?" He eyed me with open curiosity.

I shook my head.

"I'm starting to think you lived a sheltered life." He prodded for information, but I wasn't falling for it.

"Something like that." It was sweet he'd brought me dinner, but I honestly wished he'd leave me alone, because the more time we spent together, the worse it hurt that he wasn't willing to give us a chance.

He was a distraction I couldn't afford.

"I'll leave you to eat." August stood and walked from the room, closing the door between our rooms behind him.

Quieting my feelings of hurt, I ate the soup in silence, staring out the window. Night had descended, and the expanse of dark treetops seemed to extend for as far as the eye could see.

The sense I needed to hurry had continued to grow while I'd slept, until it beat like a loud, pounding drum in my head.

I needed to do something, but I was growing frustrated by not knowing what.

Setting my bowl on the table with a thunk, the chess-board rattled and a single piece toppled over. Moonlight glinted off the black knight.

Reaching out, I turned the carved horse between my fingers. What was the significance of this piece? It had been the last thing I'd seen in my vision and I'd thought maybe it was a sign to ride horseback up to the lodge, but I hadn't found any clues along the path.

Growling in annoyance, I curled up on my side on the bed, still holding the chess piece clenched in my fist.

Almost immediately, I was sucked into sleep.

4

IOLANI

My second vision was nothing like the first. Animalistic shrieks echoed in my mind, and the earth seemed to tremble around me.

Like lightning illuminating the night, disjointed images flashed in front of me. Thundering hooves. Explosive gunfire. Rage-filled faces of men I didn't recognize.

The sharp snap of a whip felt as though it lashed across my heart, leaving a stinging pain and the coppery taste of blood in my mouth.

The transition between leaving the vision and jumping back into my body was so violent I didn't have time to make it to the bathroom before getting sick. Not wanting to alert my somewhat-stalker to my plight, I tried to muffle the sounds of my retching.

When I finished, I took the blanket to the bathroom and did my best to clean it before shoving it into the dirty laundry hamper.

But the whole time, I felt as though I were being buried beneath the weight of impending loss. Time was running out and there was only one thing I could think to do. I'd follow the thread and hope it led me to wherever I was supposed to be.

Taking just long enough to clean myself up, I opened the doors to my balcony and stepped outside.

Using the metal chair as a step, I balanced myself on the balcony rail. Looking out over the ominous shadowed forest, I took a deep breath and sent my magic surging through the mental thread. I prayed it would strengthen the tentative string that was trying to guide me toward something important.

As my magic reinforced the thread, clarity hit my gut with the force of a physical punch. This was the pull of a mate.

I'd been so caught up in ignoring what was, or wasn't, going on between August and me that I hadn't recognized the pull of a second mate.

A second truth followed on the heels of the first.

My unknown mate was in danger.

For the first time since arriving on earth, I knew exactly what to do.

My wings snapped open, and I dropped from the balcony, catching a strong updraft that sent me soaring over the treetops as I rushed to my mate's side.

One hour turned to two, then three. Judging by the position of the moon, it was nearing two in the morning when I spotted fire glinting in the woods ahead of me.

Flapping hard, I rose in the sky, higher and higher until I had a bird's-eye view of the campsite far below. I studied the positions of every man moving around the camp, not wanting to risk my mate's life by rushing in, only to have him hurt in the crossfire.

There was another reason for my need to observe before acting. I had no plans for mercy. When I dropped from the sky, it would be to destroy anyone who was part of the horrors I'd witnessed in my vision. If there were any other captives, I needed to know before I turned them to ash.

Circling the camp, I searched for my mate, but the confusion of the camp made it difficult to find him. A fence was down, and horses stampeded through the camp, sending men leaping out of the way of their thundering hooves. The men cursed, brandishing weapons and calling out orders.

A group of them leaped onto the backs of the horses tied to posts near the tents and tore off into the woods. I searched the camp but saw no other signs of life, so I glided over the forest in the direction the men were galloping.

It didn't take me long to catch up. My eyes searched for what they were chasing, but other than glimpses of shadows and smoke, I couldn't make out the form of a man or beast.

That was until the woods came to an abrupt end.

The horses neighed in terror, sending up a shower of small rocks and pebbles flying around their hooves as they came to a hard stop on a flat, stone overlook. It looked like a great place for a picnic, or for plunging to your certain death.

Undeterred, the men yanked on their mounts' reins, quickly forming a semi-circle around their prey. They closed in until they were only fifteen feet from the gorgeous black horse—

No, not a horse.

The beast was so much more. His coat was black as the velvet night sky and seemed to glimmer as though it possessed stars of its own.

Eyes as blue as my hair glowed in the darkness, making it clear this creature was paranormal. Although I think anyone who saw the wide wings that hung from his back and dragged the ground would have already suspected that.

The thread in my mind glowed brighter as I studied the magnificent pegasus. He flashed his teeth at the men, slamming his powerful front hooves into the ground with enough force to leave deep impressions in the stone.

"Thought you were smart, didn't you?" One man grinned, dismounting, and walking slowly toward the trapped beast.

"I thought he was supposed to be some type of shifter, but I think our intel was wrong. He's as dumb as the rest of the animals I work with day in and day out." A second man chuckled, slipping from his saddle.

"I told you that no matter how many times you run, we will hunt you down. Dead or alive, I will drag your carcass back to camp." The first man taunted my trapped mate.

The pegasus reared, the feathers adorning his hooves moving gracefully, even as he warned the men to back off.

Mesmerized by the beauty of the beast, I forgot to watch the rest of the men.

CRACK!

The whistle of a whip rang through the air, slicing into the pegasus' side, leaving a long gash in his flank. My eyes widened as I noticed the countless other marks. Some were almost healed, but others oozed fresh blood.

He reacted by spinning around and kicking his powerful back legs at the man's head, sending the man diving out of the way.

"Shoot to maim, not to kill, boys!" the second man shouted.

Rage like I'd never felt boiled inside me, and tucking my wings tight against my back, I dove toward the earth.

Five thousand feet, a thousand feet, eight hundred feet, five hundred feet, two hundred feet.

Still, I didn't pull up. I had only one thought burning in my mind.

Death and fiery destruction.

It was time to test whether I could die and return as many times as Amaryllis… or if my death as I entered Earth was a fluke.

Calling my magic a moment before I slammed into the ground, I braced for the shock of death and rebirth.

The instant before I hit the ground, I released part of my magic, throwing up a wall of blue fire between the men and the pegasus. Then my body impacted the earth with the force of a bomb.

Men were blown off their feet and hurled into the woods. Horses screamed, bucking the remaining riders to the ground before galloping away.

Rising from the ashes, I stepped from the crater I'd created, ready for a showdown.

The men regained their footing, then cautiously moved to block me in. They kept their guns leveled on me, and I almost smiled at the confusion and terror I saw in their faces.

The man who'd taunted the pegasus took a step forward. "*What the he—*"

"I'm not from Hell, but close enough." Liquid fire was still pumping through every cell in my body. "When I'm finished here, there won't be anything left of you to send to Hades."

As one, the twenty men unloaded their weapons on me. Not wanting to risk the pegasus getting injured further, I spread my wings wide, allowing blue fire to cascade over my wings like water rippling over rocks in a river. It created a bulletproof barrier.

When the men stopped to reload, I brought my wings forward, sending hungry blue fire rushing across the dry rock and barren ground.

A whip cracked, slicing across my cheek before I could stop it. As it tore through my skin, the pegasus appeared at my side, snatching the leather in his teeth and yanking hard. The man on the other end was flung over the cliff side, where his cries went on for far too long before he reached the bottom.

Taking a deep breath, I focused on the remaining twenty-five men and sent fingers of fire streaking across the ground directly toward them. They didn't have time to even scream before my fire engulfed them, devouring them until there was nothing left, not even ash.

For a moment, the night was silent, other than the crackling blue fire that was slowly dying out. The victory was short-lived as the ground beneath my feet gave a bone-rattling groan and crumbled away.

The pegasus and I were sent hurtling toward the inky abyss below. I tried to create a plan as the world seemed to slow.

He wouldn't be able to fly, not with both his wings appearing to be broken. I knew if I shifted into my full phoenix form, I would be large enough to carry him, but there was no way I had the energy to maintain that form after the magic I'd just spent to rebirth and fight.

That left me with one option.

I'd do my best to slow our fall, and at the last minute, twist so that I landed beneath him. He should survive, and I would rebirth.

It should work.

Probably.

Dodging the falling rocks, I locked my arms around the pegasus' neck. I tightened my legs on his back and prepared to open my wings wide. Gritting my teeth, I braced myself for the pain I knew would rip through my muscles thanks to his size and the speed with which we were hurtling toward the ground.

But a heartbeat before I extended my wings, an angry shriek pierced the night and claws hooked the pegasus' back. We were yanked from amidst the falling boulders and carried out of the path of danger.

5

AUGUST

My muscles ached as I pumped my wings, trying to catch up with the blue-haired beauty miles ahead of me. I'd awakened with an ache in my chest and had known in an instant she wasn't in the lodge.

Storming into her room, I caught the soured scent that told me she'd been ill again, and my heart had twisted. I should have made her leave the door open so I could hear her if she needed me.

Her spicy amber scent led me out to the open balcony, and without a second thought, I'd launched myself into the dark sky. For two hours, I tracked her through the skies, that spark of fear for her safety shifting to confused anger.

Why hadn't she told me she was leaving? Or given me a clue about her next move?

Because you acted like an idiot and she's probably happy to be rid of your presence.

My inner voice was brutal, but probably right. I was a brewing storm cloud, while Iolani was the dewy ground after a gentle spring rain. She was full of hope and the promise of beautiful things to come, while I was cold and empty.

Why couldn't I just turn around and forget about her? That would be the best for both of us. She was safer—both heart and body—if she stayed far from me.

But there was no way I could leave until I made sure she was okay. Although I hadn't scented another presence in her room, I couldn't rule out that she'd been taken from the room by force. I knew very little about her, but I got the distinct impression this hadn't been a sightseeing trip.

She was on a mission.

Regardless of my annoyance, I'd been impressed at the speed my little mate could fly. Shifting to my gryphon form with its larger wingspan, I'd been able to cover many miles and close the gap between us. Still, it was just after two in the morning by the time I spotted her circling a mile ahead of me.

The fear that had slowly been growing in my chest faded just at the sight of her.

That relief was short-lived.

Because she'd tucked her wings and plummeted to earth almost faster than my eyes could track. It was as though she had no intention of stopping.

Had she been shot down? What if she'd had another episode and passed out?

My heart had stopped beating at the thunderous boom as her body collided with the ground and blue fire erupted around her. I blurred through the sky, pushing myself to close the distance even though I knew it was too late for me to save her.

No one survived a freefall like that.

I came to a stop mid-air, my massive wings keeping me from dropping to the ground as I stared in horror at the blue fire erupting from where she'd impacted.

My brain struggled to comprehend the truth that I'd lost my mate. I didn't even realize I'd stopped breathing until a form stepped from inside the fire and I sucked in a gasping breath.

Could it be?

Iolani stepped from the flames, like an ancient goddess of war. Her skin was bare except for the fire dancing over her like an eager pet greeting its master. Long blue hair flowed around her face as though it were made of fire.

Her mouth moved, but I couldn't make out the words. Silver wings snapped open, and my eyes widened as fire rippled over her wings without burning a single feather.

How had she survived that fall? It was impossible.

I didn't care. All I cared about was that she was alive.

So you can have another chance to ignore her and act like the backside of a donkey?

Flashes of light flickered in the darkness surrounding her, and I shrieked as I recognized the loud pop of gunfire.

She'd survived the fall only to be shot.

Pumping my wings harder, I pushed myself to get to her side, ready to protect her.

Covering the last of the forest between us, I watched as Iolani stood tall, not so much as flinching as the bullets fell around her. There was a sharp crack, the angry neigh of a horse, and I was forced to shield my eyes as brilliant fire exploded over the rocky outcropping.

I'm almost there, Iolani…

The fire was gone just as fast as it had begun. It was obviously paranormal in origin, but I didn't have a clue where it had come from or who was controlling it. When it died back, the men were gone.

I scanned the woods, but there were no signs of movement other than the riderless horses weaving through the trees, trying to get as far away from the fire and bullets as possible.

Again, I breathed a sigh of relief when I spotted Iolani standing tall, a dark stallion behind her. She'd been spared the fire's fury… and now she was going to face mine. How could she risk her life like that?

As I covered the last few feet of forest separating us, the ground gave way, sending Iolani and the dark horse plummeting off the cliff.

After seeing her crash into earth, I wasn't sure if Iolani had the strength to fly herself to safety. What if she'd injured her wing and was unable to fly?

I dropped from the sky, my body piercing the air as my eyes locked onto my target.

Iolani had maneuvered between falling boulders and was clinging to the neck of the horse. He was frantically trying to right himself, and I saw the dark wings for the first time.

Pegasus.

My shock over the impossibility of what I was seeing disappeared as the realization of what Iolani was planning hit me. Despite the size difference, she was going to extend her wings to slow their fall, even though his weight and the speed of the fall would shred her muscles. Even if she had healing abilities, she wasn't likely to fly again.

Releasing another angry shriek, I tucked my wings, easily catching up with the pair just as I saw Iolani's back muscles tense. Time was up.

My claws sank into the dark beast's flesh. I did my best not to injure him more than necessary, but I found it hard to care about his well-being when I suspected Iolani could have glided to safety if she hadn't wanted to save him.

Using the air current weaving through the deep ravine, I carried the pair clear of the crashing rocks. The pegasus was slightly larger than a Clydesdale, but his weight was nothing to me. I was large enough I could carry a helicopter for an hour or two without feeling the strain.

Anxious to check Iolani for injuries, I found the nearest moss-covered bank, and dropped the pair, before landing on all fours. Spinning around, I shifted and rushed back to Iolani's side.

I dropped to my knees beside her, pulling her onto my lap as my eyes scanned her for signs of blood. My fingers tangled in her hair, as I tilted her neck to inspect the deep slash on her cheek.

It was the only wound I found.

The scent of her blood, combined with the fear of

thinking I'd watched her die, and the rage over seeing her put herself at risk, boiled over.

My fingers tightened in her hair, and my left hand gripped her hip. "Tell me you weren't about to spread your wings and have them ripped off your back so you could save the jackass."

"He's not a donkey!" Iolani retorted, her eyes meeting mine without apology.

"I don't care what he is." I snarled, pulling her face close to mine. "Tell me you weren't about to risk serious injury for a stranger."

"He's not—" she began.

"You could have flown to safety, but you were willing to risk death for him." Our lips were so close I could taste her warm breath on my mouth.

"It would have been fine," Iolani answered stubbornly, pursing her lips, and her eyes daring me to... what? Punish her? Demand an apology? Kiss her?

Our gazes remained locked as I struggled to cope with what she'd stirred in me. Emotions weren't something I was used to, and I didn't know how to handle them.

A raspy voice broke the silence. "Are you going to kiss her, or...?"

In unison, our necks snapped up to the man standing just behind her. He was a similar height to me, but leaner. While I was built like a grizzly bear, he had the body of a sleek racehorse.

I dropped my hands from Iolani's body, only then realizing we were both naked and her bare skin was brushing against mine.

"Of course not," I answered briskly.

PDA had never been my thing, but I instinctively knew if I kissed her, it was going to become harder to walk away after I deposited her back in the safety of the lodge.

The man held out a hand to Iolani, and she tentatively placed her hand in his. "Then allow me to express my gratitude."

Pulling her to her feet, the stranger's arms wrapped around her waist, lifting her into his arms in an enthusiastic hug that made me want to kill him.

He smiled at Iolani's squeak of surprise. "Can I kiss you?"

"Ye...yes." Iolani's voice was breathy, and I was instantly irritated that it had been caused by another man.

I watched in shock as his lips captured hers in the type of kiss you'd expect to see from longtime lovers, rather than strangers. Clenching my jaw, I tried to tear my gaze away, but found I couldn't. An odd flicker of what I suspected was jealousy grew as Iolani's bare legs wrapped around his waist and his hands moved to her butt to brace her.

She was my mate.

Even if we hadn't accepted the bond, she was mine, and he had no right to touch her.

Logically, I knew I was being unreasonable, and she had every right to be touched by whomever she wanted, but that didn't stop me from standing and moving to yank her out of his arms.

"Enough!" I roared with enough ferocity to send sleeping birds tumbling from their nests and darting through the quiet forest.

Ponyboy sidestepped my attempt to yank her away and lifted a single brow in my direction. "And you are?"

"Her m—" I caught myself before the word slipped out. "A concerned friend."

A lazy smile slid across the man's angular face. "Well, then. I don't think you have any say in how I thank my beautiful mate for coming to my rescue."

His mate.

My knees buckled, but I stubbornly locked them into place, disgusted by my body's split-second sign of weakness.

Too angry to speak, I turned on my heel and strode into the forest without a backward glance.

Good. She had a mate to protect her now and I could leave without worrying about harm coming to her.

This was what I wanted.

Taking to the sky, I pumped my wings, heading toward home and trying to ignore the pain in my chest that grew stronger with every mile I put between me and Iolani.

6

IOLANI

August took to the sky, his wings sending leaves and small sticks swirling in the air around us.

I wasn't sure how he'd found me, but I was beyond thankful he'd shown up when he had. Less than five minutes ago, I'd thought he was going to kiss me, and now he'd left without giving me a chance to say goodbye.

He had to be the most confusing man on Earth. I was new to dealing with the opposite sex, but I was finding them very unpredictable. Maybe it was wiser to continue only having female friends in Cucalas.

"Do you want to go after him?" the man still holding me to him asked.

My cheeks burned as I realized my legs were still wrapped around his waist, and his palms were flattened against my bare butt.

Oh, and we were both completely naked.

"No... I, uh..." I stammered, struggling to string together a coherent sentence. "I'm not usually like this."

I loosened my legs and slid to the ground, ducking my head. What were you supposed to say when you met your mate for the first time? The man let me go, but caught my chin and lifted my face so he could see my eyes.

"So you're saying I've stirred something in you?" His grin was cocky, but his eyes held a vulnerability, a need to have me confirm I was drawn to him.

I was sure Earth women would know how to handle a situation like this. Perhaps they even have a manual for interactions between partners. I should have talked to Ryls about this.

I went with blunt honesty.

"Yes, you do. I think you're my mate, but I am new to the mate bond, so maybe I'm mistaken?" I held my breath, waiting for his reaction.

If he denied the bond, it would be the second mate this week to decide we weren't meant to be.

But his response was the opposite of August's reaction to meeting me.

"You feel it too!" His arms circled my waist, and he spun me in a circle. "I didn't think I had a mate, and had given up hope. Then a few weeks ago, I sensed your presence. It gave me a reason to live."

I smiled up at him. "That's when I came through the veil to this world."

He chuckled, pressing a kiss to my forehead. "I knew your beauty was out of this world, but I didn't think it would literally be from outside this world."

The desire to explore his body and feel his hands on

mine stole my breath. If the rustle of his feathers hadn't caught my attention, I don't know where things would have gone. Pushing out of his embrace, I moved to inspect the wings that hung limp behind him.

"What did they do to you?" I whispered, gently tracing the edges of one midnight feather.

"Until recently, there were several research facilities that ran experiments on various paranormal species. From what I gather, those were all either destroyed or dismantled by a team of paranormals." He winced as I gently inspected one of the long, thin gash marks on his side.

Not ready to have that conversation, I murmured softly, "I've heard."

"A few of the more enterprising staff members escaped, taking their favorite research subjects with them. One of those captives was me."

I circled back to stand in front of him.

"I wish I'd known so I could have found you sooner." Reaching up, I brushed my fingers across his jaw. "And I wish I could kill them again. More painfully this time."

He barked a surprised laugh. "You are an unexpected delight. For such an elegant woman, you are terrifying."

I shrugged. It wasn't the first time I'd heard that. Sometimes crap hit the fan in Cucalas and I had to sort it out. I couldn't be the nice queen all the time.

"What happened to your wings?" I prodded.

His eyes glowed with a mix of fury and pain. "They broke them. It makes it harder to escape if I can't fly. Thanks to the injections, my magic stays just out of reach and between that and the lack of food, my body can't heal itself at shifter speeds."

My stomach pitched violently, and for a moment, I considered reaching out to Hades to see if I could stop by for a visit after this mission was complete, just so I could kill the men again.

Even though my magic reserves were low, I knew I could heal him without harming myself. The thought of him being in pain for another minute longer was more than I could handle.

"Sit down and let me take care of them." I motioned for him to sit on the ground.

He caught my hand and pressed his lips to the palm. "You've done enough. I'll heal. Right now, I just want to soak in the fact that you're real and here in front of me."

I crossed my arms over my chest. "There will be plenty of time for us to get to know each other later. Right now, you're going to sit and let me take care of you."

"Bossy little thing, huh?" he teased, but obediently sat on the moss covered ground, his wings splayed out on either side of him. "What's your name? I'm Jazriel."

His name caused butterflies to flutter in my stomach. My mate's name was Jazriel.

"I'm Iolani." Kneeling behind him, I ran my hands up his back until I found the junction of his wings and his shoulder blades.

I took a deep breath and called my magic, sending it pouring into him. He gasped as the heat of my magic traveled along the length of every muscle, bone, and tendon in his body, stitching them back together with a bond that would be almost impossible to break.

Many times after a bone was broken, it was more susceptible to future breaks, but that wouldn't be the case for him. The minutes ticked by as I worked to repair the damage to not only his wings, but also his ribs, arm and ankle.

These injuries were healed, but they weren't old enough for him to have gotten them as a child. Had they purposely tried to maim him?

There would be time to learn more about what he'd gone through later. Assuming he was willing to stay with me even after learning what my future—and the future of anyone who bonded themself to me—held.

Turning my attention to his skin, I called my magic to my fingertips and traced them along every wound and bruise. I should have focused on the deep, open wounds, instead of burning through most of my energy reserves to heal superficial injuries, but I couldn't stop. Not until I'd done everything I could to ease the physical pain of what my mate had endured.

When I finished, I was exhausted, and my eyelids seemed to be made of lead.

"What have you done, my flame?" he chided, gathering me into his arms and cradling me against his chest. "I would've healed with time, but I'm thankful to be free of the pain for the first time in many years."

"You're welcome," I slurred, blinking hard in an effort to stay awake.

"Sleep. I'll watch over you." He whispered something in a language that was lost to the worlds many centuries ago, and it took my sluggish brain several minutes to translate it.

"Beat of my heart, breath of my lungs, keeper of my soul."

I WOKE to warm sunshine on my face, and birds chirping in the trees overhead. The crackling of burning wood and the scent of frying fish caused my stomach to rumble.

Arching my back, I stretched my stiff muscles… only to freeze as my breasts brushed against warm skin. Memories of the last few hours rushed through my mind, and my eyes snapped open to find a set of glowing cerulean eyes watching me with amused interest.

"Hi?" I squeaked, surprised to find him so close.

"Good morning, flame." His eyes glittered.

Sitting up, I finished stretching my sore muscles.

"I love that you aren't hiding your beautiful body from me," he purred.

"Why should I? You're my mate. Besides, nudity isn't something to be ashamed of."

Propping himself up on an elbow, he nuzzled my neck. "I can tell you it will be harder to keep my hands and mouth off you, though."

A throat cleared, and I twisted around to find August sitting beside a fire, a pan of fish frying in front of him.

I rose, wobbling for a second as a wave of dizziness washed over me. Once I was sure I could walk without stumbling, I cautiously made my way toward him as though he were a wild animal that might get spooked and dart away at any moment.

His sharp eyes narrowed and his jaw clenched. Apparently, he hadn't missed my unsteady gait. Was the man ever happy?

Stopping by his side, I swallowed my queenly dignity and bowed my head. "I didn't get to thank you for saving me... us... last night. You found me and showed up right when I needed you."

He scowled. "You could have been seriously injured or, worse, died. Why didn't you tell me you were leaving the lodge?"

Cocking my head to the side, I tried to unravel the confusing mystery that was this man. "You were planning to leave, so why did it matter when I left?"

"It shouldn't matter," August snarled, using a metal spatula to flip a golden-brown fish filet onto a tin plate. "Here. Eat. You look tired and need the energy."

I took the plate, then glanced over my shoulder at the pegasus still reclining on the ground.

"Don't worry about your lover boy. I've made enough for him. Sit and eat before you fall over," August growled.

The man was nothing but contradictions. Caring yet unfeeling. Warm but also icy cold. Tender and callous.

Obediently, I sat down on the log next to him, secretly enjoying the huff of annoyance it earned me.

"Where did you get the cookware?" I asked between bites.

August flipped two filets onto a second heavily dented plate. "After I left here, I flew over the empty camp and spotted the riderless horses. They'd returned to it, and I couldn't leave them to roam free while wearing their tack. I removed it and inspected the campsite."

It was yet more proof this man made of stone had a heart somewhere deep inside.

"I gathered supplies and decided to bring them back. I knew there was no way Pretty Boy could fly with those wings, so you'd have a long journey back to the lodge by foot. Although it appears he has miraculously been healed, so I may have wasted my time by returning."

August stood, grabbing a sack and taking it, along with the plate of fish, to Jazriel. "If I have to be in your company, you're going to wear pants."

Jazriel sat up and grinned. "Thanks, man. I appreciate it."

August returned to the log, grabbing a second pack and setting it by my feet. "You are welcome to wear clothes or not, but I thought you may be more comfortable at night wearing something since the temperatures will drop."

I didn't miss the way his eyes slid down my body before darting away. He could deny the mate bond, but he couldn't deny he was still attracted to me.

"What will happen to the horses?" I asked, taking another bite of the fish.

"We'll tell the owner of the lodge about them. I'm sure

they can send someone out to look for them. There is plenty of food and water, so the horses won't die before they can be rounded up." August took a bite of fish from his plate.

Jazriel cleared his throat. "They'll follow me."

"You can speak with horses?" I'd never met a pegasus, so I didn't know what abilities they possessed.

He shrugged. "Somewhat. It isn't like communicating with humans and is far more simplistic. But most horses will follow a pegasus without question. It's a hierarchy thing. Like wolves with their alpha."

"That's fascinating! So if we travel back to the camp, you could lead the horses to the lodge?" I asked.

"That shouldn't be a problem. How far is it?" Jazriel asked.

I glanced at August, unsure of the distance.

"It's just over a hundred miles."

Jazriel stared off into the distance. "We don't want to push them too hard, but without a rider's weight on their back every day, they should be able to make the trip in three to four days. My captors were terrible, but they kept their horses in great condition."

"I agree." August nodded. "It could take a little longer if we hit inclement weather, but otherwise it shouldn't take more than four days at most."

"You're staying with us?" My jaw dropped. "I assumed you were leaving."

August stared down at me, and I thought I saw something akin to hurt in his eyes. "I'm not that cruel. Once you are safely back at the lodge, I will leave."

My stomach twisted, reminding me how much I hated the thought of him leaving, but I wouldn't beg him to stay. Besides, it was better for my heart if he left soon, because I was afraid I was already falling for him.

It had nothing to do with the pull of the mate bond, and everything to do with his actions. His words told me he didn't want to be with me, but his actions were showing a level of care that told a different story.

"Hurry and eat so we can head out," August ordered.

Shaking my head, I turned my attention back to my plate.

7

IOLANI

I flew over the treetops, my eyes struggling to keep track of Jazriel as he darted between trees. He moved so fast it was like watching smoke and shadows.

The pegasus had wanted to rest his wings another day or two before using them and had opted to run beneath us.

My wings ached and my muscles screamed in protest, but I refused to admit how tired I still was. I'd used more magic healing Jazriel than I should have, but I would've done it again in a heartbeat.

Thankfully, once we reached the camp, I could ride back to the lodge. That would give my body time to replenish its reserves.

A large shadow moved over me, and a moment later, August's arms wrapped around my middle.

"Tuck your wings, little hawk." He pressed his mouth against my ear so the wind couldn't snatch away the words.

I hesitated, hating the idea of being a burden to him when he already found me to be an annoyance.

"Don't make me ask again," August growled.

Rolling my eyes, I did as he asked, tucking my wings tight against my back. August spun me in his arms so I was looking up at him, and our chests pressed together.

"Wrap your legs and arms around me."

This time, I obeyed without hesitation.

"Good girl." Those two words sent a delicious shiver through my body.

I was used to giving orders, not obeying them. So why did I almost enjoy it when he got bossy?

Cradled in his arms, I pressed my face against his shirt and closed my eyes. I wasn't sure I could trust him with my heart, but I fully trusted him to protect my body. For the next hour, I enjoyed breathing in his musky scent and the feel of his arms around me.

When August glided to the ground, I swallowed back my disappointment that the closeness to him was over. Unhooking my legs, I stood.

With a burst of boldness, I went up on tiptoe and brushed my lips across his stubbled jaw. "Thank you, August."

Before he could complain or push me away, I turned toward the group of almost thirty horses standing quietly, their tails swishing and eyes fixed on Jazriel.

In a trance, I circled him, admiring his sleek coat in the light of the day. He was so glossy I was almost surprised I couldn't see my reflection. He stomped his front hoof, tossing his black mane.

Stopping in front of him, I reached up a hand to touch his nose.

"Iolani! *No!*" August shouted, yanking me back.

I screamed in shock, and Jazriel reared over us, shrieking in fury.

"What are you doing, August?" I clutched my chest, trying to calm my pounding heart.

"No one touches a pegasus in this form and lives. I found the drugs the men were using to keep him sedated and his magic dampened. That's the only reason they survived, and it's the only reason his magic didn't flatten us both last night."

I eyed the pegasus, watching his hooves pound the dirt. "I think you're wrong. He grabbed the whip from the man who hit me."

August's arm tightened around my waist. "Helping you is one thing, allowing you to touch him is another. Pegasus are made of wild, untamed magic. It's the equivalent of petting a lightning bolt. All shifters are unstable at best when their animalistic sides are in control, but pegasus are nasty, vindictive beasts."

"Don't be rude! You know he can hear you, right?" I hissed.

August shrugged, not caring about Jazriel's feelings in the least. "Am I telling her the truth, beast?"

The pegasus stopped snorting and bobbed his head, mane flying.

"Yeah. That's what I thought." August chuckled, and I soaked in the rare sound. "People fear the drakons, but it is

63

the pegasus that should've struck fear in people's hearts. Their beauty is deadly."

I was finding it hard to take August seriously. It almost sounded as though he were nervous about being near Jazriel's pegasus form, which seemed laughable considering his size in both human and gryphon form.

My eyes narrowed as a new thought entered my mind. "Are you sure you aren't exaggerating just because you're jealous he kissed me?"

August huffed. "No. Believe me, or don't. There is a reason pegasus are extinct."

"What? They can't be!" I gasped, my jaw going slack. "There's one standing in front of us." Waving my hand in the sleek stallion's direction, I giggled when he did a little prance.

"And he is the first I've seen in over two hundred years. Many species have not survived the shift into modern times, and others have been hunted to extinction—like your friend Ryls' species."

"It is a tragedy that Earth is losing so many of her incredible species—of both the natural and supernatural kinds." Slipping free of August's grip on my arm, I strode to stand in front of Jazriel.

My heart raced as I reached up to stroke the pegasus' face. Not because I was afraid of dying, that wasn't a big deal for a phoenix, but because I wondered if he would accept my touch.

My hand hovered an inch from his nose, giving him

time to pull away if he wanted. When Jazriel didn't move, I gently stroked my fingers on the velvet of his nose.

August hissed a curse, no doubt expecting my imminent death.

But it didn't come.

The stallion reared back, tossing his head and snorting. Lowering my hand to my side, I watched unflinching as his dinner-plate-sized hooves stomped the ground and his wings blew my hair around my face.

Realizing I wasn't going to cower, he quieted. With a soft neigh, he lowered his head and pressed it to my forehead.

Mate.

The single word whispered through my mind, causing happiness to erupt inside me. Wrapping my arms around his neck, I laughed when Jazriel nickered and used his chin to shove me against him in a horse hug.

"I wouldn't have believed it if I hadn't seen it with my own eyes," August murmured.

Moving around Jazriel's body, I traced my fingers down his side. I'd been around horses enough to know that black horses were like black pants. They show every speck of dirt and lint. Yet, Jazriel's coat was sleek, shiny, and supernaturally spotless.

As my fingers moved across his flank, they found a ticklish spot and Jazriel's wing fluttered, smacking me in the face. My yelp of surprise turned to a laugh as Jazriel's snout prodded my ribs, finding my ticklish spot far too quickly.

"Enough, enough!" My efforts to push him away were futile.

"I'm going to gather a few more supplies, then we should get started on the return trip. Especially if the bird queen is going to stop and look at half the rocks and plants between here and the lodge." August's boots crunched across the ground as he moved away from us.

Bird queen? I knew he was teasing me over the meaning of my name, but it was a reminder of who I was and what I was here to do.

I placed a soft kiss on the stallion's velvet nose. "I'm going to go help search for supplies."

Making my way through the rough campsite, I peeked inside each of the tents. I wasn't sure what I was looking for, but hoped I would know when I spotted it.

In the third tent, I stumbled over a stash of canteens, and the fourth tent had a stack of blankets. Finding a folded piece of soft leather, I grinned and searched the tent until I found a pocket knife.

Sitting on the dirt outside the tent, I quickly cut several strips from the leather. Task finished, I cut the remaining fabric into two narrow lengths. Winding them around my feet, I used the leather strips to hold the makeshift shoes in place.

Thankfully, I wouldn't have to walk most of the journey, but it would make things more comfortable when I did.

Tying the last piece of leather, I stood and tucked the knife in the pocket of the baggy pants August had brought us that morning. As I bent to gather the blankets, a book slid from between them.

"What's this?" I murmured under my breath, picking it up and flipping through the pages.

My stomach dropped as I read page after page of notes on experiments. Most of the notes talked about subject 2447, which I quickly figured out was Jazriel, but it also referenced several other subjects.

Had they been freed when Amaryllis and her mates shut the facilities down? Or were some of them still being held captive like Jazriel?

Unbuttoning the pocket on the side of the pants, I slipped the notebook inside. I would study it later and then send it to Xerxes or Anzac. They could have their team check up on the other paranormals mentioned inside it and make sure they were safe.

August had already saddled several of the horses, and I quickly tied the blankets to one of the saddles. Hurrying back to where I dropped the canteens, I carried them to another saddle and secured them, planning to fill them when we found a stream.

"Are you ready?" August asked, striding up beside me.

"You really don't have to stay, August." I tilted my head to look up at him. "I can make it back to the lodge. We both know you could fly back to the lodge much faster than it will take us to travel on the ground."

August checked his saddle, not bothering to respond.

"I am not your responsibility." I rested my hand on his arm. "You made your decision clear the first time we met, and I've accepted your terms. If it is guilt holding you here, then just know you don't need to feel that way."

The words tasted sour on my tongue. I may have accepted that he didn't want the mate bond, but that didn't mean my heart didn't ache over it.

August's arm circled my waist, pinning me between his chest and the horse. "This has nothing to do with guilt." His lips dropped to my neck, close enough I could feel his heat, but not actually touching my skin.

My brow creased. If it wasn't the mate bond and it wasn't guilt, then why on earth was he still here? Especially when he didn't exactly enjoy my company.

Chill bumps rippled over my skin and my heart ached at his closeness and his heady scent filling my lungs.

"Then why?" I asked, voice breathy.

Instead of answering me, August lifted me into the saddle.

"If Pony Boy is ready, we should head out."

"He has a name," I pointed out, frustrated that he seemed to be toying with me.

"I know." August mounted the horse in front of mine. "I just don't care."

Jazriel trotted by us, *accidentally* smacking August in the head with his wing. At least I think it was an accident.

As Jazriel moved down the trail, the horses quickly fell in line behind him and our journey began.

THE RIDE WENT WELL that first day, right up until a squirrel scurried in front of my horse. My horse darted away from the ferocious rodent and into the woods.

Focusing on keeping my seat, I stayed relaxed and tried to reassure my mount. I didn't consider bailing. In hindsight, that was a mistake. Branches whipped my face and legs, tearing at my skin, but my only concern was calming my horse before he hurt himself.

I clung to his back as he weaved between trees at a dizzying speed. It would definitely have helped if I'd possessed my ability to open portals on Earth, and could have portaled us to an open field, but that was a skill that unfortunately I hadn't been able to use since leaving Cucalas.

None of my abilities were going to help in this situation, other than my inability to stay dead.

"Whoa. Easy. You're okay." I tried to keep my voice confident and reassuring.

The ground suddenly gave way beneath the horse's hooves. Despite my death grip, I was flung from his back. My body flipped midair, and I came to a stop when my back collided with a fallen tree in the dry creek bed.

I could have survived the tumble.

What I couldn't survive was the branch that pierced my back.

Warm liquid slid down my back at a rate that was unhealable. My magic rushed to try to heal the fatal injury, but I pulled it back, knowing it was best not to deplete myself again so soon. Especially when I was going to need to regenerate again.

Scanning the woods, I was relieved to find my horse walking around, nibbling on a patch of stray grass, completely unharmed. He was utterly unconcerned about staking me through the back, but I didn't hold it against him. He was a horse doing horse things.

Not wanting the notebook to burn with me, I worked the button and pulled it from the pocket. With my last bit of strength, I tossed it away from me. I was struggling to drag in a breath, and shadows flickered across my vision. For a moment, I thought it was a sign my time was coming, but the shadow solidified into a familiar shape. Jazriel.

The pegasus dropped his head, nuzzling my cheek, a pained sound rumbling in his chest.

"Why"—I gasped, struggling to breathe and feeling my blood soaking into the ground beneath me—"the long face?"

I don't know if he responded, because a moment later, my eyes rolled back and my muscles went slack. My body erupted into flames, turning to ash in the blink of an eye.

8

IOLANI

J ust as quickly, I regenerated.

My eyelids fluttered open to find the stallion standing motionless over me, his blue eyes wide with shock.

Behind him, I heard August's shout. I didn't want August to know what I was. If he wasn't going to be in my life, then there was no need to expose my secrets to him. It would only complicate things.

Sitting up quickly, I grabbed Jazriel's head and leaned close. "Do not tell him what you just saw. I'll explain later."

Using his front leg to steady myself, I stood. With effort, I stifled my groan of exhaustion as I leaned down to pick up the notebook and made my way over to the chestnut gelding that had tossed me like a salad.

"Hey, are you okay?" I asked, gathering the reins and walking around him to check for injuries.

August topped the hill, "Iolani! Are you ok—" His eyes widened. "Why are you naked?"

I needed an excuse and blurted the first thing that came to mind. "I took a minor tumble, and my clothes got dirty."

August snorted. "And of course the queen can't wear dirty clothes."

I ground my teeth together, but held my tongue. Opening the bag on my saddle, I pulled out another pair of pants and a baggy shirt. They smelled of the men I'd killed, and I hated it. I would've much preferred to wear nothing, but that wasn't an option.

Slipping the clothes on, I peeked at the stallion from the corner of my eye. He remained motionless, other than his eyes, which tracked my movements.

With my insides twisting into knots of worry, I walked back to him and wrapped my arms around his neck. "Once we're alone, I'll tell you everything. If you choose to leave, I will understand."

My fingertips brushed his glossy mane. With a sigh, I turned back to my horse, and took my time leading him up the embankment toward the ridge where August waited. I tried not to wince as sharp stones and sticks stabbed my bare feet.

Once we reached the top, I found the rest of the small horse herd waiting patiently for their pegasus leader to reappear. While my horse wasn't limping, I didn't want him to carry my weight, just in case. Removing the bridle, I headed toward a dark bay that was also wearing a saddle.

A gentle tug on the back of my shirt halted me. Glancing over my shoulder, I found Jazriel holding the fabric between his teeth.

"We have to get back on the trail. There is enough time to get another hour of riding in before dusk," I chided him.

Jazriel let go of my shirt, but pushed his body between me and the bay. He watched me, waiting for something.

"I don't understand." My eyes searched his, looking for answers.

Jazriel tossed his head over his shoulder, then lifted the front hoof nearest to me, holding it in place. Again, he waited.

Surely he didn't mean for me to... "You want me to ride you?"

"Oh, I bet he does," August snarled under his breath.

Ignoring him, I waited for Jazriel's response. The pegasus bobbed his head in affirmation.

Resting my palm against his side to brace myself, I carefully stepped onto his leg, testing my weight, worried I would hurt him.

With a snort, Jazriel pressed his nose just under my butt and lifted me onto his back with such ease, I was nearly tossed over his back.

He moved his wing to stop me, then pranced around the clearing, tossing his head.

"Alright. If you're done showing off, can we go now?" August snapped, moving his horse closer so he could take the unneeded bridle from my hand.

Jazriel's wings tucked against his body, holding me in place as he darted forward to become one with the shadows of the forest. Neighs rang through the air as the horses galloped behind us.

We covered mile after mile, with me perched on the pegasus' back. He was sure-footed, and he kept me nestled between his wings.

I'd expected the ride to be uncomfortable thanks to the lack of a saddle, but Jazriel's stride was so smooth, we practically floated across the forest floor. Still, I was exhausted and couldn't help feeling relieved when we stopped to make camp for the night.

Sliding from Jazriel's back, I moved to help August take the tack from the horses.

"I've got this. You look sick and need to rest." August waved me away, without so much as a glance in my direction.

It was strange how he could be so sweet, yet so rude at the same time.

But he wasn't wrong. I was barely staying upright. Dying twice in twenty-four hours had taken its toll on me.

Grabbing the blankets from the saddle, I moved away from the horses and dropped them on the ground. I curled on my side on top of the pile and closed my eyes, intending to rest for five minutes before helping scrounge up dinner. But I was sound asleep in less than a minute.

When I woke up next, I was sandwiched between two hard bodies without a clue how I'd gotten there. Trying to clear the confused haze from my mind, I let my eyes adjust to the darkness.

To my surprise, I found my chest was pressed against Jazriel's, and my back was pressed against August's chest.

What were they doing? I didn't remember a conversation about sleeping arrangements.

"Be still," August mumbled, his hand gripping my hip to stop my wiggling. "The temperatures are dropping and we're keeping you warm."

My heart did a weird fluttering thing that made it hard to breathe. They were taking care of me?

They had no idea that I didn't need their warmth, but it was the thought that counted. The leaves overhead rustled as a cool night breeze wafted across us.

Jazriel groaned in his sleep, and resting my hand on his arm, I found his skin cool to the touch.

I might not be cold, but they were. Wanting to repay the care they'd shown me, I called my magic. I used it to stoke the fire in my chest until it heated my skin.

Jazriel responded instantly, scooting his body tight against my front so fast that it shoved me into August.

August's chest rumbled with a growl, and I wasn't sure if it was from annoyance at the disruption to his sleep, or if it had something to do with the hard length that pressed against my backside.

I stiffened in surprise, and August's fingers dug into my hip. Was he aroused?

A different kind of heat stirred far lower in my body. It was ridiculous how quickly my body responded to theirs.

"Mmm." Jazriel drew in a deep breath and his hips rocked forward almost imperceptibly.

Just that tiny movement caused August's length to grind harder against my butt.

I flushed, trying to pull back the heat I was radiating. I'd wanted to warm the guys, not cook them alive.

Jazriel's mouth found mine. Unlike the sweet kiss of the first night, this one was hungry and demanding.

His hand slid under my shirt, moving across my bare ribs and stopping just beneath my breast. Was he giving me time to stop him? If so, he needn't have bothered. I was pretty sure I was going to burst into flames if he didn't touch me more.

Not caring if it was too forward, or unladylike, I placed my hand over his and slid it upward. Jazriel didn't need to be asked twice, and he eagerly cupped my breast.

I whimpered, unable to imagine anything on earth could have felt better. He swallowed the sounds of my pleasure, his hard erection bumping against my belly.

His continued hip movements were causing my butt to grind against August's manhood, and while the latter was silent, I hadn't missed the way his body had gone taut. The gryphon shifter gripped my hip as though it were the only thing keeping him grounded.

When Jazriel's thumb brushed my nipple, an electric charge sizzled through me and I arched into his touch. In the darkness, Jazriel's eyes glowed, and his fingers began working magic, touching and teasing my breast.

My stomach twisted with unfamiliar sensations, and something feral began demanding release as heat rushed between my thighs. I wanted to touch Jazriel, but I'd never touched a man intimately before. What if I did it wrong?

I'd listened to the phoenix women on Cucalas reminisce

about time spent with their mates, so I wasn't clueless about how mating worked, but it was different acting on it.

Jazriel must have sensed my hesitation because his fingers moved to where mine rested just under the hem of his shirt. Curling his fingers around my wrist, he pressed my palm against the lean muscles of his stomach.

Pulling his mouth from mine, he whispered, "Please touch me, my sweet mate."

August pulled me ever so slightly away from Jazriel, his chest rumbling. Surely he couldn't be jealous since he was the one who didn't want me.

Jazriel responded by pressing harder against me. August growled, his hard length grinding against my butt. Blood pounded in my ears, and my body ached in newly awakened places and I wasn't sure what to do to satisfy the need gnawing at my insides.

"Flame, are you trying to kill me? Your scent could drive a man to do crazy things," Jazriel groaned.

"What kind of things?" Thanks to my inability to take a deep breath, I sounded breathy, like an old movie starlet from the movies I'd binged the last few weeks.

Grabbing my thigh, he pulled it over his hip, allowing me to feel his hard length as it pressed against my aching slit.

"Some people are sleeping," August growled.

His voice sounded annoyed, but the twitch of his erection against my butt said otherwise.

"Good. Then keep sleeping." Jazriel's perfect white teeth flashed in the darkness, then his mouth found mine again.

His hips began a steady rhythm, and I swore shooting stars were falling around us.

"Oh!" I whimpered as shock waves of pleasure spread through me.

Behind me, August's breathing was rough and his hand had slid from my hip, up to my ribcage, only stopping when his fingers brushed the underside of my breast.

Heat spread from where his fingers touched my skin, causing my nipples to harden. I wished he would move his hand to massage the sensitive mound, but I was too proud to ask.

My fingers trailed across Jazriel's chest, enjoying the lean, taut muscles. He shifted positions slightly, grinding against my most sensitive spot, and I gasped, my nails digging into his skin.

He repeated the motion, heat and mischief glittering in the depths of his glowing eyes. My lips parted, but no sound came out. Jazriel took that as his sign to continue the agonizing, delicious torture.

That feral thing in my belly grew more demanding, twisting my insides into knots and turning my thoughts into a jumbled mess. Faster and faster, the pegasus male rubbed against me until the need built to a terrifying level.

August's breathing was growing harsher as my body slid across his erection. His thumb brushed the underside of my breast, sending heat rushing between my thighs.

Gasping, I tried to wiggle from between them before I hurt them. "I'm going to explode."

"Good," Jazriel purred, his fingers digging into my thigh to keep me in place.

"You... don't understand," I pleaded. "Something is building inside me. I... I think something is wrong."

"Nothing is wrong. Trust me." Jazriel placed a soft kiss on my lips. "Give in to the feelings."

And so I did. Letting the thing inside me grow, I needed to release it, but I couldn't seem to let go.

Until August's hand slid on my sweat-slick skin and cupped my breast. I thought it was an accident and he would move it away... but he didn't. His fingers gently massaged the tender flesh, while his thumb teased my nipple.

It was the final push I needed and sent me hurtling into bliss.

My moan filled the quiet night air as my release tore through me. I quivered as intense aftershocks continued exploding inside me, one after the other.

Jazriel hissed my name, while August's breathing had turned raspy. Both men stilled as they joined me in ecstasy, their burning lengths jerking against my sweat-soaked skin.

If making out was this amazing, phoenix or not, I wasn't sure I could survive actual sex.

9

IOLANI

The following morning, we took advantage of the nearby creek to wash away the sweat and evidence of our nighttime activities.

August was extra growly, refusing to even make eye contact. Jazriel was the opposite, barely able to keep his hands off me. There was no denying I loved it, but I knew I needed to talk to him before the physical intimacy went too far.

My chance came when we reached a place where the trail narrowed to the point the horses had to follow in a single file line. Jazriel was in the front, and August, who was still quiet, had chosen to bring up the rear.

"I know you can't answer me, but there are things about me you need to know." I ran my fingers through his mane, enjoying the silk strands against my skin.

The pegasus turned to look at me, human intelligence shining in his eyes.

"I'm a phoenix."

For the first time since I'd been riding on his back, Jazriel stumbled.

Unsure if that was a good or bad sign, I decided to push ahead. "I'm Iolani, Queen of Cucalas—the phoenix afterlife. There was an incident where I ended up in this world. Unfortunately, that caused the veil between the two worlds to become unstable. I think if I returned to Cucalas, it would restore the balance and repair the veil. But I can't go back yet. The spirit of a dark phoenix escaped from Cucalas and is loose on earth."

I paused, taking in a deep breath. "Azurea has to be stopped before she finds a host body that can hold her."

When I fell silent, Jazriel squished me between his wings in an odd sort of hug.

My fingers stroked his feathers. "To complete my mission, I need to increase my power. Apparently, bonding with mates will give me that needed power. But as much as I need that power to defeat Azurea and handle the veil, I don't want to bind someone to me for only that purpose. I'm not even sure I can take my mates through the veil with me.

"I want to take a mate because it's something I never dreamed I'd get to have. That type of relationship and intimacy is something I want to share with a mate for the rest of my life."

Jazriel ruffled his feathery wings, his ears forward as he listened to me spill everything.

"I don't want us to claim each other, and then you wonder if I was just using you. If this isn't the life you wanted," I steadied my voice, "or if I'm not the woman you want, then I want you to know I will understand if you walk away."

The pegasus shook his head, tossing his mane.

"Jazriel, please don't stay with me out of guilt or thinking you owe me anything for the night we met. I've survived one mate not wanting the mate bond, I can survive another." Leaning forward, I ran my hand down his neck. "I don't even know where I will be when the veil is closed between our worlds. My life isn't normal, so chaos is all I have to offer you for the foreseeable future. And my heart."

He shifted from beast to man, twisting around and catching me in his arms. It was fast and so smooth that I was left gaping up at him. "I accept."

"What?" I asked, my mind still reeling to comprehend his quick shift.

"You offered me a life of excitement and adventure. Why wouldn't I want a life with a fiery mate with a fearless heart and the sexy body of a goddess?" His lips sucked and kissed their way up my neck.

It wasn't until that moment that I understood how scared I'd been that Jazriel would make the same decision as August and walk away from me. Although that wasn't quite accurate, since August kept claiming he was going to leave, but never seemed to follow through.

My heart swelled with hope. "Jazriel, you can take all the time you need to think—"

"I don't need time. My decision is made. You proposed,

and I'm not letting you take it back." He teased, catching my bottom lip between his teeth and giving it a playful suck before releasing it.

"But I didn't—" I began, only to be cut off when he shifted back to his pegasus form in the blink of an eye. Once again, I found myself sitting astride his back.

"How did you do that?" I asked, knowing I wouldn't get an answer.

Jazriel pranced in response, his neck tall, tail lifted, and hooves high-stepping.

I giggled, my heart feeling light for the first time since I'd arrived on earth. "You are such a showoff."

My laughter excited something in the pegasus, and he continued to alternate between prancing and trotting for the next few minutes. When his stride lengthened to a gentle canter that had my body rocking on his, I realized I was in trouble.

I gasped and immediately closed my mouth to hide any further noises. But the stallion slowed to a walk, turning his head to study me. My cheeks burned and a knowing glint entered his eye.

"Jazriel, whatever you are thinking about, don't—" I warned, but it fell on purposefully deaf ears.

With a wild toss of his head, and what sounded like the horse version of laughter, Jazriel lunged forward. He imme-diately fell back into that dangerous loping canter.

This time, he didn't hold me in place with his wings. Instead, he held them out to his sides, allowing my body to roll against his powerful muscles beneath me.

It was beyond embarrassing how quickly that feral need built inside me, and it was a matter of minute's before my legs gripped his sides, hissing his name through clenched teeth as I rode out what I realized must be an orgasm.

He didn't immediately stop, and I climaxed a second and then a third time. My eyes closed and my body trembled as I clung to him. Jazriel finally took mercy on me and returned to his smooth, floating gait, tucking his wings against my limp body.

A soft caress brushed my mind, and I heard him whisper. *Body. Soul. You are mine.*

AUGUST SPENT the remaining days of the trail ride alternating which horse he rode on to ensure they didn't become overexerted. Despite my efforts to convince August my fall hadn't been bad, I could see in his eyes that he wasn't buying what I was selling. For once, the two men agreed on something, and I was only allowed to ride Jazriel for the remainder of the trip.

I'd rolled my eyes. Was this what Ryls had to deal with her mates? I was fairly close to invincible, yet they were treating me as though I were a glass doll. August didn't know my identity, but I had a sneaking suspicion it wouldn't have changed his stance in the slightest.

The third day, I was once again lifted onto Jazriel's back. I'd spent the previous night cradled between the men, but to my disappointment, there were no repeats of the first night's activities.

The long hours on the trail without having to guide my mount gave me the opportunity to read through the notebook. Tears slipped down my cheeks as I learned the truth of Jazriel's treatment.

Countless injections, breaking of bones every time he attempted to escape, the horrific ways they'd tried to force him to shift so they could torture his secrets from him. Through it all, Jazriel never broke. He never shifted to his human form, and he'd refused to show them any of the abilities he might possess.

I'd healed the outward signs of his decades of torture, but I didn't know how to help with his inner scars. By the time we stopped to camp our final night, I was emotionally drained from what I'd read and imagined.

August dismounted beside us and stretched his back. Jazriel shifted, catching me in his arms and cradling me to his chest.

"There is a river ahead. The horses are too tired to cross tonight, so we'll make camp here." Jazriel set me on my feet. "I'm going to go check it out and find the safest place to cross."

August nodded in agreement. "I'll come with you. It shouldn't be hard to grab a few fish from the river for dinner as well."

Jazriel blew me a kiss and the two men disappeared into the woods. Once they were out of sight, I pushed to my feet and began removing the saddles from August's horse and the rest of the horses who were carrying our gear. The guys were going to fuss about me exhausting myself, but I couldn't stand around waiting for them to take care of me.

I'd just finished starting a small fire and setting the frying pan next to it when I heard a woman cry out from the woods. Standing up, I turned toward where I thought the sound had come from and strained to listen.

Again, the pained cry came from the woods. Without thinking twice, I rushed toward it. As I darted between trees, I would pause every few minutes to listen for the woman's cry, and each time it was closer.

Was it an injured or lost hiker, or could someone be keeping her captive? With woods as untouched as these, it wouldn't surprise me to find out some people used the wildness for nefarious purposes. Just like the men who'd held Jazriel.

I'd braced myself for just about every possible scenario, except the one where a mountain lion emerged from the thick undergrowth with its claws extended. She slammed into me, sending us tumbling to the forest floor, where the big cat lunged for my throat.

I could've turned her to ash with a burst of flames, but I didn't want to injure the magnificent creature for doing what she was built to do. Calling flames to my hand, I waved them in front of her snarling face, and sighed in relief when she leaped away with a roar.

Not ready to give up on having me for dinner, the mountain lion circled me, her eyes reflecting the blue glow of my fire. Pushing to my feet, I began to back away. The oversized kitty cat stalked after me, her tail flicking in irritation.

Keeping my voice soothing, I tried to reason with her. "I swear phoenix doesn't taste like chicken."

She hissed, closing the distance between us. My wings ripped through my shirt, and I turned to leap in the air, but the cat was fast and her claws sank into my back and her sharp fangs bit down where my right wing met my shoulder.

I screamed as agony tore through my wing. Gathering my magic, I sent a small burst of electricity through her, hoping it would be mild enough to only stun her for a moment so I could escape.

It worked, and she dropped from my back so fast that I staggered…

Then tumbled end over end down a rock-covered bank…

Before finally crashing into a rushing river.

I was quickly sucked beneath the surface, where my wings got caught in the violent current, making it impossible to resurface. My efforts to shift were futile. I simply couldn't focus with my body slamming into submerged boulders and my wings feeling as though they were being ripped from my back.

Managing to break the surface, I sucked air into my oxygen-starved lungs. A heartbeat later, I was yanked back beneath the water. I continued to fight the powerful river, cursing my inability to portal myself away.

My lungs began to burn and my muscles grew weak,

warning me I was running out of time. But my battle ended a moment later when my head impacted against a boulder with a sickening crack. My body went limp as death claimed me.

The only thing worse than drowning in a river was regenerating underwater to find you need to fight for your life. Again.

Without my wings pulling me down, I kicked hard and managed to break the surface.

Just in time to catch a beautiful view of the golden hour sun turning the river gold as I toppled over a waterfall.

10
AUGUST

Iolani's cry echoed through the valley and sent ice water through my veins. Before the sound stopped, I'd already shifted and taken to the air. Jazriel shifted and, using his wings, he ran across the river's surface below me.

Fear weighed heavily in my stomach, a sensation I hadn't experienced before meeting Iolani, but was becoming a common companion these days. Trouble seemed to follow the blue-haired bombshell wherever she went, and I was considering tying her to me just to get through a day without chaos.

My gryphon's eyesight allowed me to see Iolani stumble from the woods that ran along the river. Crimson marred her skin, but I couldn't understand what had caused the injuries. Not until she turned to run, and a large mountain lion jumped on her back. It tore into her wings and skin with claws and fangs.

I shrieked, alerting the stallion to the situation. We both

pushed ourselves to reach her before our delicious mate became a literal snack.

Iolani glowed, then the cat dropped to the ground, buying us time to close the distance. Or so I thought.

My heart stopped beating as she staggered, falling down the steep embankment and splashing into the river where she disappeared.

Jazriel was foaming at the mouth at how hard we were driving ourselves. Still, I watched in shock as he dug deeper, lowering his head, his form seeming to dissipate into wispy shadows as he streaked across the river's surface.

Surging forward, I hurried after him, all the while my eyes scanned the rapids, searching for any sign of Iolani. Her head burst from the churning water, but just as quickly, she was gone again.

My eyes caught a flash of blue under the water, but it disappeared as fast as it had appeared. No, no, no. She had to be okay.

I shrieked with relief when her head resurfaced again, but it turned to a pained cry when she fell off the side of the earth.

A waterfall.

Jazriel didn't slow, launching himself over the edge. Together, we tucked our wings, diving toward the jagged rocks below, all the while searching for any sign of her. We hovered over the rocks at the base of the waterfall, thinking maybe she'd gotten hung up on one of them.

From the corner of my eye, I caught another flash of blue

down the river from us. Turning, I stared in shock as Iolani crawled onto the riverbank.

My wings went weak, and I nearly dropped into the river myself. By some freaking miracle, she was alive and appeared to be unscathed.

Jazriel's furious battle cry had me searching for the cause of his hurry. That's when I spotted the large grizzly bear barreling toward the tiny female, who was still on her hands and knees, spewing up water.

The bear roared, and she finally looked up.

Rather than screaming in terror, she groaned as though she was facing an inconvenience rather than imminent death. "This day can go suck a duck."

Jazriel reached her first, standing over her body and bracing for the bear's impact.

I went straight for the bear just as his claws cut through the air toward Jazriel. Sinking my talons into his back, I hauled him into the air. Fury and fear warred inside me, and I struggled with how to handle my rising emotions.

"Don't hurt him!" Iolani shouted, crawling out from beneath the pegasus.

I hovered mid-air, unbothered by the angry, six-hundred-pound animal swiping at my underbelly. What did she want me to do with him? Take him back to camp for a tea party? This wasn't a teddy bear.

"He's just a bear doing bear stuff." She stood, wobbling on her feet.

Yeah, so? I was a killer gryphon doing angry gryphon crap.

"Please, August. Just set him down a little way from here. We can leave before he comes back. This is his home. We crashed it."

Pinning my ears against my head in annoyance, I caved and flapped my way a half mile from Iolani and gently dropped the livid grizzly on the ground.

By the time I returned to Iolani, Jazriel had coaxed her onto his back and, with a soundless beat of his wings, he joined me in the sky. Rising above him, I glided just over Iolani's head, studying her for signs of injury. I was still in disbelief that she'd survived.

Reaching up, she brushed her fingers through my belly feathers. A purr rattled in my chest before I could stop it.

"You're adorable, feathered feline." She grinned up at me, and warmth spread through me despite the ridiculousness of the pet name.

This woman had the cheat code to my emotions, and it was going to be the death of me.

WE RETURNED to the camp where I found that the stubborn female had not only removed the gear from the horses, but she'd spread out our blankets and built a fire. She should have been resting while Jazriel and I took care of things.

I headed back to the river. With my restless energy and stirred-up emotions, it didn't take me long to catch enough fish to feed us. Shifting back to my human form, I took my time cleaning the fish. I tried to rid myself of the annoying feelings that continued to linger, but it was useless. Giving up, I strode back to camp.

Jazriel stood from the blankets where he sat with Iolani and took the fish from me. "You hunted, I'll cook."

Accepting help wasn't something I enjoyed doing, but I handed him the fish without protest. I strode straight to Iolani's side. Since meeting her, I'd been able to avoid giving in completely to the instinctual pull of the mate bond. It had been hard, but doable. But I was facing a new problem.

I was falling for her, and it had nothing to do with being mates. Sure, I still felt the link between us and my inner beast was pushing for me to claim her, but this was different.

Giving into my heart, I dropped to the blanket. I pulled her into my arms, closing my eyes and relishing the comforting warmth of her body that assured me she was alive. She was safe.

Iolani didn't protest or question me. She simply let me hold her.

Slowly, my tumultuous emotion bled away, leaving me feeling almost normal. I should have released her after she'd calmed the mess she'd stirred inside, but I couldn't.

"Dinner is served!" Jazriel appeared with a cheeky grin on his face and set a plate overflowing with fried fish on the blanket between us.

Breaking a bite-sized piece off a filet, he popped it into Iolani's mouth.

"You two know I'm an adult, right? I've run a kin—" She paused, stumbling over her words. "I've been in charge of the well-being of thousands. I'm pretty sure I can feed myself."

Jazriel brushed the back of his knuckles across her cheek. "I know. But we are allowed to enjoy taking care of you."

I snorted. "Honestly, I'm not sure how you've stayed alive this long. You would've become dinner for a bear if we hadn't shown up. I think Amaryllis' legendary knack for dancing with death has rubbed off on you."

Iolani twisted around on my lap to look up at me with fire blazing in her eyes. "I would've come out of that unscathed."

Her utter confidence in what she claimed had me laughing until my sides hurt. Jazriel leaned back on his elbows, watching me with open amusement as though I were making a fool of myself. Iolani set her jaw, looking as though she wished she could burn me to a crisp. But as I wiped tears from my eyes, her anger faded and her features softened.

Reaching up, she trailed her fingers along my jaw. "You're so beautiful."

"Just what every man wants to hear." I chuckled, catching her hand, and pressing a kiss to the palm before I could stop myself.

Iolani's eyes widened with surprise, and I wanted to kick myself. For showing too much affection... and for not showing her enough.

If I was going to leave, I needed to do it soon. It wouldn't be fair to allow the bond between us to grow stronger, only to cause her more pain when I disappeared. I was cruel, but not evil. Still, I wasn't strong enough to walk away right then. I needed her in my arms.

"Eat," I ordered, picking up a piece of fish and touching it to her lips.

Her eyes never left mine as she opened her beautiful lips and let me feed her. It was intimate, almost more so than that first night she'd slept between Jazriel and me. The night he'd given her what seemed to be the first orgasm of her life.

I had found her first. Even if we hadn't completed the bond, I was her mate and it should have been me who'd shown her pleasure. But it had been the pegasus, her second mate, who'd had the honor.

He had accepted the bond without question, and my sweet Iolani had returned it with an open heart and arms.

Just like how she would accept you if you stopped being such a fool, my inner voice pointed out.

That night was burned forever in my memories. She'd quivered between us, her spicy, sweet scent heavy in the air, my hand cupping the petal-soft skin of her breast, and her rounded butt grinding against my cock. I'd come in my pants like a horny college student who'd never touched a girl in his life.

Jazriel had been focused on giving her pleasure. But when he'd realized I was awake, I'd seen his smirk and the glint in his eye. His movements had caused me to hump against her until I'd grown painfully hard. It humiliated me to realize I was so easily aroused by her, but I hadn't possessed the willpower to walk away.

I hated him for it. But I hated him more for not initiating something similar the following night.

Earlier that afternoon, I'd caught the lingering scent of her arousal on the trail. Jealousy had surged through me, and I'd fought the urge to shift and pluck her from his back. I wanted to carry her into the skies and show her the pleasures of mating thousands of feet above the earth.

Gryphons didn't share mates. Trevor had confided in the pride that he struggled with sharing Ryls in the beginning. So why wasn't I angry at having to share her with Jazriel? Probably because I saw how easily he could bring a smile to her lips, and I would do anything to see her happy.

My resolve was growing weaker by the hour. It was selfish, but I wanted to claim Iolani as my mate. I was experiencing the stirring of emotions now, so maybe I could offer her more than a cold, unfeeling heart. But I didn't know if that would be enough. Especially now that she was experiencing what it was like to have a mate with unbridled emotions and passions.

Gryphons only had sex once they found their fated mate, so it had never been something I thought about. Now I spent my days harder than granite while imagining all the things I could do to hear her scream my name.

I wanted to claim every inch of her skin with kisses.

I wanted to taste her mouth, her skin, her sweet cream.

I wanted to hear her whimpers and feel her tremble with release after release.

I wanted to be her protector. But what if my callous nature caused me to be the one to hurt her heart?

When we finished eating, I resolutely set my jaw and moved her from my lap to the blanket. Then I headed into the woods without a backward glance, knowing I wouldn't be able to stop myself from trying to show her how badly I longed to be given a chance at being worthy of her love.

11

IOLANI

My heart sank as August's face hardened and his eyes shuttered. He went from the gentle guy I was falling for to the powerful warrior I was also falling for. Why did he keep putting up the wall between us?

I wanted to cry, but I refused to show my weakness over a man who kept running from me.

"He's arrogant, but he'll come around." Jazriel wrapped an arm around me, pulling me against his side.

"I don't think so. He's forced to be around me right now, but once we get to the lodge, he will be gone."

Jazriel laughed. "You don't force a man like August to do anything he doesn't want to do. He is aware I can protect you as well as he can, but yet he's still here."

"I don't understand why he thinks he has to protect me." I picked at a loose string on the blanket.

"Maybe because you haven't told him what you are?" Jazriel suggested, reaching up to ruffle my hair. "He might be less afraid if he knew you were the mother-clucking queen of the phoenixes. See what I did? Cluck? Because you are a bird?"

"Seriously?" I wrinkled my nose. "It's a good thing you're cute, because your puns are lame."

"You think I'm cute?" He slipped his finger under my chin and turned my face up to his.

My cheeks warmed, and I batted his hand away. "That's an understatement."

Grabbing the notebook I'd left on the blankets, I flipped it open.

"Will you ever tell him?"

Resting my chin on my palm, I stared into the woods and considered Jazriel's question. "No. August is a man of honor. If he thought we were fated to be together so he could aid me in battle, he would accept the claim without question. He would risk death for me, he just isn't willing to risk falling in love with me."

"But he would fall in love once you two bonded." Jazriel intertwined his fingers with my free hand.

My throat tightened, and I shook my head, unable to speak.

Jazriel's thumb stroked in gentle circles on the back of my hand. "But you don't want him to love you out of duty or because of the mate bond."

"No," I whispered. "And I won't ask him to risk his life for me. It's hard enough to ask for your help."

"Technically, all you've mentioned needing from me is the energy that comes from the mate bond"—his eyes twinkled—"and I assume from sex. Lots of sex."

"Jazriel!" I yelped.

"What? I'm more than happy to offer my services." He bent, brushing a kiss across my lips, then pulled back. "Which reminds me, I've been thinking, and I believe I can help. How much do you know about pegasus?"

"Very little." I motioned toward the notebook in my lap. "And it seems despite how long you were held captive, they didn't learn much about you either."

Jazriel's eyes hardened, then an easy smile spread across his face. "I refused to let them win. My only entertainment was watching how angry I could make them."

He laid back on the blanket, pulling me down and into his arms. "Now, let me tell you about my idea."

Curling up against him, I stroked my fingers across his chest.

"Like Icarus, pegasus are drawn to fly as close to the sun as possible. But unlike Icarus, we gain power from it. We are at our weakest during the brief moments of darkness during complete solar eclipses, while solar flares and solar storms supercharge us."

"That's amazing!"

Jazriel's eyes glowed with pride. "Thank you, Flame. There is a solar storm happening now, and in two days' time, it should be at its peak. If you can replenish your magic by then, I can use those flares to funnel more power through the bond and into you. I don't know how long until the next storm like this will happen, so this may be our best shot for a while."

My heart soared with hope. "You can do that? Without harming yourself?"

Jazriel nodded. "I've done it many times. In fact, I used it the night I sensed how close you were. That's when the flares started and I used the burst of energy to burn through most of the drugs in my system and break free."

"This might work!" Happiness bubbled in my chest, and then I glanced at him through my lashes, feeling suddenly shy. "You were coming to find me?"

Jazriel grimaced. "I was giving it my best shot, but I miscalculated how bad of a condition I was in. When they trapped me on that ledge, I thought it was all over. Then a blue meteor streaked from the sky, turning the tables in an instant. Talk about making an entrance! Your presentation is sharper than a unicorn's horn." He rolled onto his back, pulling me on top of him.

"I was happy I made it in time, but I wished I would have known sooner."

"My precious little mate, you came exactly when I needed you." Catching my face between his palms, Jazriel kissed the breath from my lungs.

When he pulled away, his face was serious. "You died that night, didn't you?"

"Yes. I was determined to reach you before they started firing, and my fury made it hard to think clearly." I rested my head against his warm skin.

"Were you planning to die again if August hadn't shown up?" His chest rumbled against my cheek.

Reluctantly, I admitted, "I was going to cushion your fall."

"You're one crazy, brave woman. How'd I get so lucky?" His fingers trailed down my spine. "August believes you survived by pure luck today. But I want the truth. How many times did you die?"

"Twice." I chuckled. "I regenerated just in time to be there as I tumbled over the falls to my second death. Worst timing ever."

Jazriel rolled, tucking me beneath his body. His eyes glittered with a mixture of amusement and exasperation. "You find that funny? I knew you could regenerate, and I was terrified. But poor August didn't have a clue, and I thought I was going to end up with giant bird crap on me the whole time I ran below him."

"I think he was more frustrated at being inconvenienced than concerned about my safety," I murmured.

"I'm a selfish man, and it's in my best interest to let you believe that so I can keep you to myself. But you're wrong. August is terrified of the things you make him feel. He sees himself as your mate, and he thought he'd lost you today." Jazriel brushed the loose strands of hair from my face.

"How could you know that?" I reached up to trace the curve of his lips, but pulled my hand back at the last second and rested it on my chest.

"It's a gift, you could say." Jazriel winked, then caught my hand and brought it to his lips. One by one, he sucked each of my fingertips into his mouth, speaking between kisses. "Now, tell me why you keep holding yourself back from touching me."

"You're supernaturally beautiful. I'm new to touching and being touched, and it's intimidating to initiate it with you." Biting my lip, I kept from adding, *and I can't believe you are attracted to me.*

"Just as you are mine, I am yours." Jazriel leaned down to brush his lips against mine. "I want to feel your touch as often as you are willing to give it. Nothing is off-limits, and for the record, I love PDA."

My forehead creased, "PDA?"

"Public Displays of Affection," Jazriel explained. "I want everyone to know I'm yours and I'm happy to show off—it's a pegasus thing. We have zero embarrassment."

"I thought pegasus didn't like being touched." This time, when I reached up, I traced the line of his lips.

"That's true of anyone other than our mate." Jazriel's tongue darted out to lick my finger. "You can touch me whenever and wherever you like. But yes, I will kill anyone else who touches me."

I shivered at his nonchalance. It was easy to forget that behind his beauty was a merciless beast who made even a mountain of a man like August nervous.

"Tell me what you need to recover from regenerating. I imagine it takes a lot of energy, and you've done it multiple times." Jazriel placed soft kisses along my jaw.

Make love to me, I thought, but didn't say it out loud. "My belly is full. Now I just need to rest."

"Tell me the truth." Jazriel's mouth moved to my neck, sucking and licking.

My laugh was breathy, and my pulse jumped. "With food and sleep, my magic will replenish itself."

Was it possible there were faster ways to recharge? According to Ryls, yes. But I wasn't about to ask for that.

He trailed kisses along my collarbone, moving down. His mouth stopped just above the swell of my breast.

As though it had a mind of its own, my back arched, trying to encourage him to move just a little more.

"The truth, Iolani." His voice lost its characteristic playfulness, becoming commanding. "Tell me what you need from me."

His warm breath blowing across my skin made it hard to think about anything other than having him fill the ache between my thighs. "Jazriel, I... want you."

He rumbled with satisfaction. "If we do this, it is likely my beast will claim you." His hand moved to my throat, angling my face toward him. "I'm not going to be able to stop him because I want the same thing. Are you sure you want me as your mate?"

"Yes. Yes, I'm sure." Wrapping my legs around his waist, I pulled his hips against mine. "Please, Jazriel. Mark me, mate me, claim me."

He needed no further encouragement, and his mouth devoured mine. Supporting himself on his elbows, he slipped his right hand under my hips, holding me tight against the searing heat of his erection.

"Jazriel!" Wet heat rushed between my legs and my belly grew heavy with need.

His lips moved to my breast, sucking the hardened nipple into his mouth. Rolling his hips, he used the hand on my butt to slide my aching slit against him.

That wild thing in me began to pace, demanding release. Sinking my fingers into his shoulder-length dark hair, I pulled his mouth from my breast and back to my mouth. The thread binding us together seemed to glow in my mind, and the drive to be claimed by my mate added fuel to the wildfire burning through my chest.

My slick arousal coated him as he continued to stroke against my entrance. As my need grew, it quickly turned painful.

"Flame," Jazriel hissed through clenched teeth. "Your first time should be special, tender. But I'm not going to be able to keep my beast at bay. I swear I'll make it up to you for the rest of our lives."

"If you don't shut up and fill me, I'm going to experience my third death today by burning alive," I snarled.

One second, I was looking into Jazriel's glowing blue eyes, and the next, I was on my hands and knees looking down at the blanket.

"Oh!" I breathed, shocked at the dizzying speed with which he'd shifted our positions.

"OOH!" I screamed as his length entered me in one hard thrust.

He tore through the thin barrier and buried himself deep. My fingers curled in the blanket and I tried to squirm away from the searing pain, but his fingers dug into my hips, holding me against him.

"I'm sorry, beautiful. I'm so sorry." Jazriel leaned over me, murmuring apologies and brushing kisses across my shoulders. "Be still, my love. Give your body a chance to adjust."

I whimpered, torn between the desperate need still curled tight in my belly and the sharp pain shooting from where he was buried inside me. His right hand slid over my hip and down my belly, stopping when his fingers found where our bodies were joined.

When he found my clit, my muscles trembled, and I gasped. He said nothing as his fingers worked magic on my body. I could do nothing but moan as the pain receded and the feral need began to grow.

I rocked back against him, encouraging him I was ready for more. Jazriel's hands moved back to my hips, and he pulled himself out inch by inch. I didn't even have time to miss the fullness before he buried himself inside me again. My eyes crossed at the pleasure-laced pain that rippled through me.

Jazriel's control must have completely snapped, because I could do nothing but try to remember to breathe as he thrust into me. My knees were lifted from the blanket as he angled my hips to thrust deeper into my tight heat.

Stars sparkled in my vision, and I felt dizzy as my body rushed toward a terrifying release. Jazriel must have sensed how close I was because his rhythm increased until our skin was soaked with sweat.

I lifted my eyes, trying to focus on anything to keep me grounded. What I spotted was August leaning against a tree at the edge of the woods. His eyes glowed as our gazes locked, but his face remained impassive. He looked completely unconcerned that he'd been caught watching.

What worried me was how my body reacted. My lust reached a boiling point, and with my eyes still focused on August, I climaxed, screaming until my voice was hoarse. Wave after wave of erotic bliss slammed into me, stealing my breath and causing my muscles to tighten around Jazriel's erection. It was more than he could take and he roared my name, his body jerking as my walls continued to milk him.

August turned, storming into the woods, and I couldn't blame him. Although I knew in my heart if he hadn't put the wall between us, we would have already claimed each other.

Not wanting to feel the hurt that August's leaving caused, I glanced at Jazriel over my shoulder. My heart skipped a beat at the raw lust and feral hunger on his face.

He was untamed and wild.

And he was mine… my mate.

Blue tongues of fire licked across my skin as magic swelled in my chest.

"Gorgeous." Jazriel reached out a hand, holding it just in front of the fire, as though he were asking permission to pet an unfamiliar dog.

My flames responded to his curiosity by rushing across his skin, consuming both of us in a blue column of fire.

Setting my knees back down, Jazriel tucked his left arm around my waist and moved the fingers of his right hand to my throat. He gently pulled me toward him until my back was pressed against his chest.

His wings appeared, wrapping me in a feathery cocoon as I tilted my head back against his shoulder and his mouth claimed mine. My leg burned as his magic marked me. Glancing down, I found a trail of hoofprints running up my outer thigh. I was forever his.

Tears blurred my vision, and I wished with all my heart I could mark him like Ryls had marked her mates. I wanted the world to know he was mine, and if they touched a man bearing my mark, they would know to pray that death found them before I did.

To my shock, I watched the column twist and swirl as though caught by a breeze. Jazriel turned me in his arms as we watched it sparkle and dance over our heads. Slowly, a crow-sized bird made of fire emerged. The bird landed on my shoulder, eyeing me for a long moment before giving me a quick nod of its head.

My jaw dropped as it spread its wings and flew directly into Jazriel's chest. He hissed in pain, but to his credit, he didn't release me or try to get away.

When my fire slowly faded away, my mouth went dry as I stared wide-eyed at the image of a phoenix emblazoned across his chest.

"So... how do you feel about tattoos?" I asked belatedly.

12

AUGUST

I'm not saying I hate that horse, but if he's ever hit by a bus... I'll be the one driving that bus.

13

JAZRIEL

The sun was high in the sky as I smelled the scent of humans a few miles ahead. My pegasus recoiled, pinning back my ears and slowing my pace. I didn't handle the scent any better than my beast, and fought against the instinct to turn and gallop in the opposite direction.

Pegasus weren't known for associating with other species on our best days, and nothing in the last couple of hundred years in this world had made me want to change that. I knew my species had their faults, but we also had a strict moral code.

Humans were willing to do anything to get what they wanted.

I was the last of my species. Our ability to roam had been restricted, thanks to the hunters who saw us as trophies, or a status symbol for their estate. Those who hadn't been killed in a hunt had their souls die because of being confined to ever smaller areas of land out of reach of most humans.

We were not meant to be tamed, and when we were finally broken, both our souls and bodies died.

Now I was heading toward a human dwelling, and everything inside me screamed I should turn around.

But I didn't because of my mate, who trusted me enough to lie on my back and fall asleep. I was careful to keep my wings pressed tight on either side of her body so she wouldn't roll off.

It was strange having weight on my back as I'd never been ridden. Even in my drugged state, I'd killed all five men who'd tried to break me during my captivity. And their deaths had been violent, bloody deaths that had earned me weeks of torture.

I was over five hundred years old, and I'd never heard of a pegasus accepting a rider. Then again, I'd never heard of a pegasus coming down off their high horse and taking a mate of another species. Which was likely another reason my species had vanished from existence.

I'd always considered myself unlucky because I was too stubborn to just give up and die like the rest of my brothers and sisters. How wrong I'd been. Getting to meet my mate was worth everything I'd survived.

I wouldn't have cared what she was—gryphon, shifter, wizard, human—I would have loved her the same. Well, maybe not unicorns. Those uptight pricks had sticks shoved so far up their butts, they stuck out of their foreheads.

But being matched with a phoenix was the last thing I'd expected. Especially since I thought we'd made the critically endangered species list around the same time.

I'd heard the chatter among my captors about the unstoppable tiny phoenix who was basically like a ninja, but with unconventional battle techniques. Personally, I'd thought they were exaggerating. But after seeing the power Iolani had displayed when she'd destroyed every man on the cliff without breaking a sweat, I understood their fear.

Over the past few days, I'd had plenty of time to study and learn about my mate. Should I have told her I could read the minds of most paranormal creatures? Probably.

But after years spent in my pegasus form, I'd become better at gathering information by observing and listening. Humans lacked magic, making it difficult to use my magic to listen to their thoughts. I could gather bits and pieces if I focused hard enough, but it was often garbled and made little sense.

I thoroughly enjoyed listening to my mate's rambling thoughts. She was incredibly sensitive and tender-hearted for a being of her power.

Her mind was filled with thoughts about Cucalas, her kingdom, her love for lumberjack-looking decor, her battle with Azurea, and her worries about the upcoming challenges. She feared nothing except failing those who counted on her.

Secretly, I'd loved her thoughts about me. And yeah, I was that vain. She spent a lot of time admiring both my human and pegasus forms. There had been an unforeseen downside to my ability to read her mind, though. When her mind turned to replaying our kisses and reliving what she'd felt when she'd been squished between August and me, my body couldn't help but respond. I'd never spent so many hours rock hard.

By the time she confided what she was, I'd already known. She'd thought my shock when I'd found her in the woods had been from watching her die and rebirth, and while I had to admit that was one lit party trick, it hadn't been the reason for my surprise.

That had come from the unfamiliar magic I'd picked up in the air. It was a magic I hadn't sensed before, so I knew it wasn't hers or August's. I'd tasted it in the air more than once on this trip, and I was beginning to wonder if Iolani's freakish brushes with death weren't accidents. But I wasn't going to add to her worry until I was sure.

While pegasus sucked at sharing, I found myself wishing August would hurry up and accept the claim so I could confide my suspicions. I wouldn't betray Iolani's trust by revealing her secrets unless it became a life and death situation. But I would've felt better if he'd been aware of the situation so he could be prepared for any attacks.

Where Iolani's mind was painted in color and filled with beauty, August's was hostile and monochrome. Or at least that's how it had been before Iolani. With each hour he spent in her company, I was seeing his mind's stark landscape shift to a drab wash of color.

He was seeing and feeling the world differently because of her... and his butthole was puckering in terror. Which was a problem, since the man had never experienced fear and was doing his best to distance himself from it.

That first night we'd slept with Iolani between us, I'd

wanted him gone. But Iolani's thoughts keyed me into the fact he was her unclaimed mate. When I realized he'd walked away from her, I'd given serious thought to killing him for hurting her heart. Then her thoughts had shown me how he'd been there for her and my desire to have my mate happy and safe outweighed my desire to kill him... which was saying a lot, because I really wanted to kill him.

Sharing a female wasn't a pegasus trait. We tended to kill any rivals for our mate's attention; it was simpler that way.

My opinions changed when I realized how turned on she'd been by having August involved during intimacy. Anything that added to her pleasure was something I wanted.

Which was why, when I'd sensed August moving through the woods, I'd made sure to angle her so that she faced him. And as expected, when she'd spotted him watching us, her lust had spiked.

Intimacy with the pair of us increased her pleasure to a level we wouldn't be able to achieve separately.

So until the winged pussycat stopped being a flying chicken, I was going to take every chance to show him what he was missing. I enjoyed goading him, and I adored pleasuring her... so it was a win-win situation for me. Because the sooner he came to the realization that he could never walk away from her, the sooner we could start showing our beautiful mate a whole new world of pleasure.

Speak of the devil and he shall appear...

"The lodge is just past that line of trees." August

trotted up next to me. "How do you want to handle this? Do you want me to take her and give you time to shift and come up when you're ready? I can also open a balcony door for you and you could come in under the cover of darkness."

He might not read minds, but he'd picked up on my discomfort and was trying to make this less stressful for me. It was disgustingly sensitive for a man who thought he was too cold to love.

Coming to a stop, I tossed my head toward my back.

August understood. Pulling his horse to a stop, he dismounted and gathered Iolani into his arms. His arms bumped my wing, and he stiffened. He turned wide eyes on me, waiting for me to retaliate.

I snorted.

He belonged to Iolani, so he was safe. But I wasn't about to tell him that. I hated people feeling comfortable enough to talk to me... the last thing I needed was for them to feel comfortable touching me.

As August stepped away, I flicked out my wing, whacking him in the back of the head. He grunted, whipping his head around to glare at me. But I had both my wings tucked tight against my back, and I widened my eyes in feigned innocence.

"You, my friend, should've been swallowed," he hissed, walking away like he'd had the last word.

Yeah? And I bet your baby toe gets banged more than you do.

August spun on his heel to face me. His eyes narrowed as he tried to figure out if he'd imagined my voice in his head, or if his imaginary friend had developed a sense of humor.

I blinked, acting as though I couldn't hear the delightful string of curses running through his mind.

Color me impressed! Who knew he was so creative? I struggled not to laugh, knowing it would confirm his suspicions and ruin my future fun.

"My mistake. I thought I was dealing with an adult," he mumbled, turning toward the lodge and striding away.

Poor, naïve man.

August had done the worst possible thing you could when interacting with a pegasus…

He'd amused me.

And I was going to take advantage of every opportunity to push his buttons.

SEVERAL HOURS HAD PASSED by the time I slipped on the clothes August had left, and strode from the woods. I might've stayed hidden until dark if not for spotting Iolani reclining in a chair in the courtyard.

She was holding the notebook she'd taken from my captors' camp, and once again, I kicked myself for not burning the book when I had the chance.

The last thing I wanted was for my mate to read what I'd been put through or about their plans to create a breeding program with me as the stud. They believed I'd jump at the chance for sex and female companionship, but I'd refused to shift to my human form and had ignored the captive female paranormals and eager human volunteers they'd shoved into my pen.

Recently, they'd concluded I lacked a human form, and had shoved female horses in heat into my tiny electrified cage, hoping my biological needs would win and I'd mount them like the animal they thought I was.

When that had failed, their conversations had turned to finding a way to collect my semen. The only reason it hadn't happened was because no one had been brave enough to jack off the beast who killed every man who'd touched him. Sure, sometimes I had to wait until the drugs wore off a bit, but they'd all died.

I hadn't touched any of the females, but I worried my mate would feel disgust—or worse, pity—for me when she read those entries. Her sensitive heart was determined to locate the other captives mentioned and ensure they were safe, and that alone kept me from making the book disappear.

My eyes searched the lodge grounds that were visible from my hiding place, looking for threats to Iolani's safety. But other than the two humans working to get all the new horses groomed and settled in the barn, the lodge was nearly desolate.

A guy had checked in shortly after we arrived, and a woman had joined Iolani on the patio area. The two had exchanged greetings, and then the woman had opened a novel and started reading. Every few minutes, the woman would burst into laughter, then quickly read the line out loud, and their giggles would echo across the valley below.

The sound was irresistible and drew me forward.

Iolani sensed me coming, and a beautiful smile spread across her flushed face. "Jazriel! There you are!"

Sitting down on the lounge beside her, I forced her to scoot and give me room.

"There were other chairs." My mate giggled, and I found myself entranced by this version of her.

Now that she'd been fed, slept for hours, and had the energy from our bonding surging through her, she practically glowed.

Why hadn't I realized how drained she'd been sooner? Because she was as stubborn as August and good at hiding any signs of weakness.

"I prefer this seat." Tucking my arm around her shoulder, I pulled her close and kissed the top of her forehead.

Iolani rolled her eyes, but her body leaned into mine and she sighed happily. "Belle, this is my—"

Noticing her panic as she tried to find the word, I jumped in. "I'm her fiance, Jazriel."

I knew I should offer to shake hands, but it was a human custom I would need time to adjust to. While I might learn that you couldn't kill someone over a handshake, my inner beast was going to take a while to convince.

Belle didn't seem bothered by the lack of a handshake. "Iolani mentioned her boyfriend, but didn't tell me she was engaged!"

Sliding her glasses down her nose, her eyes flicked down my body, lingering for a moment at the low V of my shirt where part of the phoenix was visible.

I laughed. "She's a bit shy about it because she proposed to me."

"Way to go after what you want! I'm here for it." She winked at Iolani, then looked back at me and explained, "Iolani and I have been laughing over some of the cliche descriptions of the sexy men in this book, and she claimed you fit those descriptions. It turns out she wasn't lying."

Iolani blushed, and I fought the urge to strut. Pegasus had legendary egos, and having my mate stroke mine was an incredible high.

"I'm just lucky she gave me a second look." Lifting Iolani's hand to my lips, I placed a soft kiss on the back.

"It's clear you two were meant to be together." Belle smiled and tucked her book into an oversized tote at her side. "I'm going to my room and pretend one of my book boyfriends is real and curse the universe for not giving me a sexy hunk."

"I hope we bump into each other again, Lani! It's been forever since I had the chance for some girl talk." Standing, she wiggled her fingers in a small wave and headed inside the lodge.

"She seems so nice. It was like bumping into an old friend." Iolani turned and smiled up at me. "But I'm glad it's just us now. I missed you."

Her thoughts slid through my mind, images of how she wanted to straddle me, grab my face between her hands, and kiss me. How she wanted to feel me inside her, filling her as she rode me as if she'd stolen me and needed to make a hard and fast getaway.

I was getting hard just from her thoughts, but she simply tucked her head against my chest. It was cruel, even if it was my own fault for eavesdropping.

Pulling her onto my lap, I caught her face in my hands and kissed her like it was the first time. When I released her, she was panting, and she had the sexiest bedroom eyes I'd ever seen.

She adjusted herself on my lap, inadvertently grinding against my painfully hard erection. "How much time before you expect the solar storm to reach its climax?"

The only word I heard was climax.

"Wh...what?" I asked, my heart tripping as she leaned forward to wrap her arms around my neck, which had her soft breasts so close to my face I could nearly lick them.

Since we'd met, I'd only seen her wear the oversized men's clothing, or my favorite—nothing at all. The tank top she was wearing fit her like it was painted on, and her breasts looked ready to spill over the top at any moment. It was tempting me in ways I hadn't experienced.

I wanted to rip her top down and mark her breasts with kisses and gentle bites. Just like I wanted to unzip my jeans, reach beneath her flowy skirt, push aside the strip of fabric between her thighs, and bury myself in paradise.

Temptation was an invitation I never refused, but I didn't want my beautiful mate to think I was an animal who couldn't control himself, so I did my best to focus on what she was asking.

"How long before I need to be ready to work on the veil?" she repeated, while the fingers of her right hand brushed idly through my hair.

"Two nights from tonight," I answered, trying to breathe through my mouth so I wouldn't smell the sweet scent of her arousal.

My inner pegasus would see that as a sign of our mate having needs we were neglecting, and I'd end up taking her right there on the patio, not caring who might happen to wander by.

"So soon," she whispered, leaning forward and tucking her face in the crook of my neck.

Her warm breath on my neck, combined with the fingers running through my hair, and her other hand trailing down my chest, had me swallowing a growl. She was killing me.

I'd hated being touched, and now I couldn't get enough of being petted, and was two seconds away from begging for belly rubs like a pathetic dog.

Oh, how the mighty had fallen.

"Do we need to travel somewhere special where you can reach the veil?" I asked, my voice husky.

She shook her head. "I can touch the veil wherever I am on this side. When it comes time to trap Azurea in Cucalas, I will need to return to the spot where we traveled between the worlds. The veil is weakest there, so it will be the easiest spot to open and send her back."

126

"One thing at a time. First, we stabilize the veil. Then we'll figure out how to handle Azurea." I traced my fingers along her spine.

"Thank you for being here for me. It's nice not being alone." Iolani shifted positions so she could suck my bottom lip into her mouth.

I nearly exploded in my pants.

"We need to get you fed and back into bed," I croaked, fighting every fiber of my being that told me I should selfishly take what I wanted.

"I've slept enough." She laughed, then wiggled her hips playfully. "Besides, I'm comfy here."

Well, that makes one of us, I thought, wanting her to stop moving but simultaneously wanting her to move more.

"The amount of power I will be funneling into you is going to take everything you have. I need you to focus on saving every bit of energy you have over the next two days." Wrapping my arms around her, I held her to me, reassuring myself she was strong.

"If I go upstairs, will you cuddle me?" Her eyes held a naughty glint, but her thoughts were serene and sweet.

I would have agreed to anything this woman asked of me, so I nodded. "Only if I get to be the little spoon, though."

14

IOLANI

I grabbed my shoes from beside the door. Tiptoeing out into the hall, I gently closed it behind me. Jazriel was still sleeping, and after the show-stopping performance he'd given me and the follow-up encore, he deserved to sleep in.

My night would have been perfect if August had been with us. But I hadn't seen him since he'd carried me into the lodge the day before. I tried to tell myself he was just tired and was sleeping like a rock, but I couldn't completely silence the voice that was telling me he'd left without a goodbye.

The long hours of sleep, combined with my mate's incredible stamina, and my anxiety over August, had left me buzzing with so much nervous energy my skin crackled with tiny electric shocks every time I brushed against something.

I needed to run, and thanks to the suitcase filled with

clothing and shoes Ryls had delivered while I'd been on the trail, I had the proper shoes to enjoy it.

Once outside the lodge, I stretched and then started jogging along the trail marked as being the easiest. My long strides quickly turned to a run, and within minutes, I felt the tension in my muscles fade.

Ahead of me on the trail, I caught movement. Slowing to a walk, my eyes made out the form of a man sitting on a log on the side of the path.

"Good morning!" I called out to the man sitting on the side of the trail. "Everything okay?"

The man gave me a lopsided grin. "I'm fine. Just a little dizzy. I guess I'm not used to running at this elevation."

"It can take some getting used to," I commiserated, although my phoenix shifter side made altitude of little concern for me.

The man's chocolate brown eyes squinted up at me. "Hey, aren't you Iolani? I was planning to come find you when I got back to the lodge."

"Um, yeah?" I answered, hesitant to answer this complete stranger, even though there was an odd sense of having met him before.

"Sorry! That sounded so creepy." The man smacked his forehead in an exaggerated gesture. "I'm Thom, and I was sent by Xerxes—well, Ryls. She threatened to come here herself if Xerxes didn't send someone to help watch your back. Did you get the suitcase I left for you at the front desk?"

"That sounds like Ryls. She's a firecracker when she gets

an idea in her head." I chuckled. "And yes, thanks for the clothes! I traveled light since I knew I would ride up to the lodge. So how'd you get an entire suitcase up here?"

Thom shrugged. "The weather cooperated yesterday morning for a helicopter to fly up here. After dropping the gear, I rappelled down."

He stood. "If you're ready to head back to the lodge, I'm good to jog again."

"Sounds good!" I grinned, and let him set the pace before following into step beside him. "So when do you leave?"

"Whenever you tell me to, boss lady," Thom wheezed, clearly still struggling with running in the thin mountain air. "I'm on permanent loan until either you're finished with your work, or until you get tired of me and send me packing."

"I hope you're being paid to do this." I winced, hating that he was being forced to help me.

"Don't feel bad! I volunteered. It beats cleaning up the mess at Xerxes' home and military base in Mexico." He shot me a smile that, combined with his boy-next-door good looks, would've had most girls hurrying to drop their panties.

But although I felt a connection to him, I didn't feel the pull of the fated mate bond. Plus, I had my hands full with August and Jazriel. The last thing I needed was a third man in the mix.

As we rounded a corner on the trail, we came face-to-face with a moose. I didn't know if it was a male or female, but I didn't think it really mattered. Not when it was almost two feet taller than me at its shoulder and its antlers were almost wider than I was tall. Plus, it appeared the only thing this moose hated more than mornings was humans.

"We need to back away very slowly." Thom's hand grabbed my arm, and he pulled me backward.

The moose charged, closing the distance between us with an almost paranormal speed. I didn't want to injure the beast unless there was no other choice, but I also didn't want Thom to get stomped into a pancake.

Shoving Thom out of the way, I ran toward the moose. At the last moment, I veered to the side and shot down an animal path and away from the main trail. The moose took the bait and changed direction to chase me.

I ran through the woods, weaving between tree trunks and ignoring the thorns yanking at my hair and cutting my skin. When I was sure Thom would be well out of the moose's line of sight, I turned and ran back to the main trail, planning to spread my wings and take to the air.

But as I raced back onto the trail, I was rammed in the side by what felt like a freaking boulder. My body flew back in the direction I'd just come, sliding across the ground and into the underbrush. I didn't even have a chance to call my magic before a large hoof cracked down on my head.

Over and over, the two moose stomped and kicked my crumpled body. Ribs cracked, and I shrieked as my ankle and forearm shattered under the weight of the hooves. Each time I tried to call my magic, another sharp blow to the head caused me to lose focus.

I'd just closed my eyes to wait for the death blow I knew was coming when a strong wind surged down the trail, whipping up dirt and leaves. An ear-drum piercing shriek of raw fury seemed to come from everywhere around me.

Opening my eyes. I watched as the large gryphon dropped to the ground, still screaming at the moose. He wrapped the talons of one of his massive feet around me, not crushing me, but making it clear he was claiming their kill.

How lame. The only way I'd been able to get the sexy gryphon to claim me was to look like roadkill. I'd learned a lot about weird human kinks during my time on Earth thanks to the internet, but this was a new one I wasn't really sure I could get down with.

Bellowing in annoyance, the moose slowly backed into the woods.

The moment they were gone, August shifted.

"You really suck with animals, you know that?" His voice was rough, but his hands were gentle as he practically scraped me off the trail.

"I noticed. Really sucks, since I wanted to be one of those princesses who had animals singing to her and cleaning her house." I laughed, then regretted it as pain ripped through my chest.

Closing my eyes, I called my magic and sent it searching for the damage.

Footsteps pounded against the pavement. "Is she okay?"

"She's alive," August answered bluntly, making it clear he wasn't interested in a conversation. Then his voice dropped, and he whispered, "I should spank your perky little backside for this. Why would you go out alone?"

I couldn't answer. Partly because I was weirdly intrigued by the idea of being spanked by him, and also because I was dying.

The only problem was, I didn't want to die and regenerate in his arms. That was probably the fastest way to expose my secret.

"That thing came out of nowhere!" Thom stared at me, his face pale as he strode beside August. "Are you okay, Iolani? You saved my life!"

"Well, she shouldn't have, and if she dies, I'll kill you too," August snarled, his lip curling.

"Stop it. This wasn't his fault." I tried to hide how difficult it was getting to breathe, thanks to the blood slowly leaking into my lungs. "Thom was sent here by Xerxes to help me with… stuff."

"Well, maybe he should've started by helping you stay alive." August wasn't in the mood to be reasonable, and I didn't have the energy left to argue.

Hooves pounded down the path, and a moment later, the pegasus shoved his face next to mine. Bingo. He was my ticket to saving my secret.

Focusing on the link between us, I sent my thoughts flooding into his mind. *Listen, I know you can read minds. Do NOT shift to your human form.*

Jazriel's head reared back in shock. *There's no way she could know that—*

I cut him off. *I figured it out on the trail and confirmed it yesterday on the patio when you were getting turned on by the thoughts I sent to you. So don't even try to deny it.*

He still didn't believe me. *Okay, but that doesn't mean she can read my thoughts…*

I rolled my eyes and then groaned as knives stabbed my skull. *Yes, I can. Now shut up and listen. I'm dying, and if I don't get away from August in the next couple of minutes, my cover will be blown. Follow my lead.*

Jazriel whinnied, and his ears dropped.

"August? Every step is jarring and hurts so bad," I gasped, not needing to pretend to be in pain thanks to the horrific pain of bones grinding together and internal bleeding. "Please let Jazriel carry me on his back. It will be smoother and hurt less."

August didn't even question my request and quickly settled me on Jazriel's back. The pegasus eyed me with anguish. I'd hidden my plan from him, but he still sensed he wasn't going to like it.

"Let's go, Pony Boy. We need to get her to the lodge and slow the bleeding to give her time to heal," August snapped, and began to run alongside Jazriel, leaving poor Thom to bring up the rear.

Okay, there's a large pond alongside the trail right before we exit onto the lodge's property. I need you to buck me off. Aim for the pond, I told my mate while using just enough magic to keep my heart beating.

You want me to kill you? Absolutely not.

I'm already dying. I promise I'll be dead before I hit the water.

Ha! And what do you expect me to tell August?

Tell him you stepped on a bee or some crap like that. He'll be so relieved I'm healed, he will not think twice about you.

I might be a jerk, but I'm not that heartless. Find another way.

My vision was darkening, and we were nearing the pond. We were running out of time and it was now or never. *I'll make this up to you later. Now, aim for the pond.*

WHAT?

I sent magic surging to his butt, giving him a non-fatal shock.

The pegasus screeched as the muscles in his hindquarters spasmed, sending me toppling toward the pond that ran alongside that part of the trail.

Yee-haw!

MY PLAN WORKED BEAUTIFULLY.

I sank below the water's surface just as I turned to ash, and regenerated a moment before August dove in after me. He yanked me to the water's surface, where I sucked in a breath of fresh mountain air.

"I'm going to turn that horse into glue." His tone was murderous, but his eyes were soft.

He started to step from the pond, then realized I was naked, and paused, his eyes scanning my body. "Where did your injuries go? And your clothes?"

Okay, so I didn't think that part of the plan through.

"Maybe they were those fun ones that dissolve in water?" Jazriel suggested with a smirk.

I glared at him. "How do you know so much about this Earth when you were in captivity for so long?"

Jazriel sat down on the grassy bank, not caring that he was nude, and grinned. "It's amazing the stuff people talk about when they think you're a dumb animal. Not to mention how many movies I watched over my guards' shoulders as they streamed movies and shows on their phones."

"Why did you call it 'this Earth?'" August asked, and I could practically see him trying to put all the pieces of the puzzle together. "You make it sound like you're an alien."

Hoping to distract him, I feigned a shiver even though I wasn't cold. "May... Maybe we should talk about this once I dry off?"

"Hm." August turned to eye Thom, who'd politely turned away from the pond. "You can return to the lodge."

"Thom's here to help me with my work. Ryls and Xerxes sent him," I told both of my mates.

"I don't care who he is, no man is going to see my ma —" His eyes widened, and he tried to hide it. "*You* naked."

"I saw her naked," Jazriel volunteered, licking his lip as he looked at me. "You have no idea what you missed last night."

Why did he always pick the worst times to goad the gryphon?

August turned his back to Jazriel and ran his hands over

my skin. Magic sparked between us, and I caught my breath at the unexpected intimacy.

"You are completely healed." August stated the obvious, not ready to let it go. "That shouldn't be possible. Even the strongest species would need hours to heal the fatal injuries you healed in seconds."

I tried not to notice the way his soaked tee was clinging to his broad chest. "My magic is stronger after I've eaten and slept."

"And don't forget riding this pony's bony. That definitely helped," Jazriel called helpfully from behind August.

"Does he ever shut up?" August closed his eyes, and his lips moved as he counted to ten. He was somewhat less murdery-looking when he opened his eyes.

Seeing that Thom had taken his advice and disappeared to the lodge, he sat down on the bank, pulling me onto his lap as he continued searching my body for injury. "Is he telling the truth? Does sex give you power?"

"Yes." There was more to it than that, but I wasn't ready to give him details.

"What are you, little bluebird?" His fingers brushed over Jazriel's mark, and I thought I caught a flash of pain in his eyes.

His fingers moved up my belly, where they slid between my breasts.

I caught my breath. "Are you going to stay with me?"

August didn't respond. He seemed in a trance as his fingers trailed across every inch of my skin except the parts that burned to feel his touch.

Catching my chin between his finger and thumb, he brought his mouth so close to mine that his lips brushed featherlight against mine.

"Dude. Stop driving us all crazy and just freaking kiss our girl!" Jazriel snapped.

I swallowed my pride and pleaded, "Please stay with me."

August slowly released my chin and leaned away from me. "I can't."

My eyes filled with tears, and Jazriel was there in an instant, lifting me into his arms.

"You better take good care of your eyes, since they are the only set of balls you possess," he spat at August, then carried me toward the lodge without a backward glance.

15

IOLANI

After we'd returned to the lodge, I headed to the suitcase to find something comfortable to wear. My body had flushed with embarrassment when I found the selection of garments Ryls had packed for me to sleep in. Things I didn't remember buying and wondered why she thought I'd be needing them.

I'd finally selected one that seemed to have the most fabric and headed into the bathroom to try it on. To my surprise, when I'd slipped it over my head, I discovered the fabric was sheer and gauzy.

My skin had turned a brighter shade of red than Ryls' hair, as I stared at my reflection. Every inch of my skin was visible beneath the fabric. It covered my butt—barely. If I bent forward even the slightest bit, my entire backside would be exposed.

Somehow the garment screamed "screw me" louder than if I were wearing nothing.

I couldn't wear this.

Reaching for the hem, I prepared to pull it over my head. I hesitated at the soft knock on the door.

"Yes?" I asked.

"I know you plan to take it off, so I just wanted to see you in it first." The door wasn't locked, so he could have just come in, but he'd asked, sensing I was uncomfortable.

It was that display of respect for my feelings that had me releasing the hem. So what if I looked like I was begging my mate to take me to bed? There was no shame in him knowing that, or in purposefully trying to arouse him.

Taking a deep breath, I'd opened the door and watched in delight as Jazriel did a double take.

"Hades," he hissed, devouring my body with his eyes.

Emboldened by his reaction, I pushed him backward onto the bed and crawled over him. His pupils dilated, and his breathing was rough.

My hand slid along his length, and my excitement grew when his entire body shivered. It had been a while since I felt powerful and in control, and I'd forgotten how much I liked it.

It was time to do something else I wanted, and explore every part of his body... with my mouth.

"SO WHY DIDN'T you tell me you could read minds?" Jazriel asked.

We were lying on the bed with my head resting on his chest and my leg tossed over his.

I laughed. "Because you were having too much fun being nosey, and then I found it hilarious when I realized I could send you mental images and you had to pretend not to be affected."

"That's mean." Jazriel tickled my ribs. "Have you been able to read my thoughts from the beginning?"

"No. In Cucalas, I can hear the thoughts of many people, but many of my powers seem to be out of my reach here on Earth," I admitted. "It was after we completed the bond that I could hear you if I focused. I can also block thoughts, but I find that harder to do with you. Maybe it's the mate bond?"

"What other abilities do you have?" Jazriel asked, brushing his fingers up and down my bare arm.

"I'm going to keep that as a surprise. We don't want you to get bored with me," I teased. "Besides, now that you've boosted my energy levels, I have to test my abilities. I'm not even sure what I am capable of now."

We fell into companionable silence, until Jazriel asked, "When this is all over, where do you hope to be?"

"I honestly don't know. All that matters is that balance is restored, and I'm with you."

Jazriel kissed my lips. "I'll take that."

I plucked up the courage to tell him what had been weighing on my heart all afternoon. "Jazriel? I think the animal attacks aren't random."

His hand stilled. "What do you mean?"

"It's possible that Azurea is manipulating them." I rubbed my eyes. "If she can kill me before I stabilize the veil or before I trap her, she would be free to do as she pleases without worrying about me."

"Do you think she has enough power to do that?" His voice had lost its playfulness.

"Maybe. I'm the only one who was strong enough to beat her."

"Even if she is behind the attacks, what would she hope to achieve? You will just regenerate," Jazriel pointed out.

"But if she takes me out enough times in a row, I could be weakened to the point my magic is too weak to allow me to regenerate. Or she might be planning to try and possess my body."

"Who wants to possess your body?" August's deep voice asked.

I sat up, pressing my hand to my chest, and stared at the man leaning in the open balcony doorway. "August!"

How long had he been there? How much had he heard?

"I was just saying I thought the moose wanted to take me out." Even to my ears, it sounded ridiculous.

"Or animals just don't like you?" August suggested, raising an eyebrow.

"It's a shame we can't ask the moose." Jazriel twirled a lock of my blue hair around his finger. "Did he give you his name, by chance?"

"Of course not!" I wrinkled my nose at his silliness.

Jazriel nodded sadly. "It makes sense that he'd want to remain anonymoose."

I groaned and August moved to sit in the chair as though too exhausted by Jazriel's nonsense to keep standing.

"Animals don't put out hits on humans or paranormals." August leaned back in his seat, spreading his legs and folding his arms behind his head.

My temperature spiked, and my mouth dried.

Are you imagining yourself in his lap, riding his cock like you did mine last night?

I hadn't been, but now that Jazriel put the thought in my head, I was finding it hard to think of anything else.

That man has it bad for you, little flame. Imagine how he'd react to you dropping to your knees between his legs—

"Animals can be controlled with magic, though." I tried to refocus on my conversation.

"So you think he was *moose-guided* by dark magic?" Jazriel's dead-pan delivery almost made me laugh at the lame pun.

"What? You didn't find that *amoosing*?"

"Enough!" Grabbing a throw pillow from the bed, I straddled his chest and pressed it against his face, pretending to smother him.

Under the pillow, Jazriel promised to behave, so I lifted it, eyeing him with suspicion.

"Maybe you didn't think it was funny because you *moosed* the punchline?"

"What is wrong with you?" I smothered him with the pillow again.

Jazriel's muffled cackling got to me, and I started to laugh too.

When I pulled the pillow away, the emotions in his eyes hit me like a punch to the gut. He was doing his best to be there for me. Using the idiotic humor to distract August from asking questions I didn't want to answer, to distract me from my anxieties over Azurea, and to ease my hurt over August's continued denial of our bond.

He was trying to be my everything.

I leaned forward until our noses nearly touched, and rested my palms on either side of his face. His chuckles died away as he searched my face for the cause of my tears.

Then I whispered three little words into his mind. *I love you.*

Jazriel's reaction caught me off guard. He placed a soft kiss on my lips, then rolled to his side and tucked me against his chest.

"If you two are going to nap, I'm going to go find food for Iolani." August stood and walked toward the adjoining door.

"Thank you, August," I called.

The hard man simply nodded and closed the door behind him.

"Are you okay? I didn't mean to upset you." I brushed my fingers through Jazriel's hair.

"I'm beyond perfect, beautiful mate. I just need time to process this, and I want to do it while holding you." Jazriel's voice was deeper than I'd ever heard.

Content in his arms, and a little sleepy from yet another

regeneration in a matter of days, it wasn't long before I fell asleep.

THE AFTERNOON WAS SPENT LOUNGING. I felt lazy, but Jazriel reminded me that the success of our plan depended on me being at my peak. Secretly, I think the men were just trying to keep me in the room so I wouldn't get attacked by birds or mauled by wolves.

August disappeared and reappeared throughout the afternoon, bringing various trays of snacks and dishes. I didn't miss the way he watched which items I reached for first, and which I avoided. He was trying to learn my likes and dislikes, which made no sense if he was leaving me.

More than once, I'd caught his gaze drifting over my body when he thought I wasn't looking, and I hoped he would act on the undisguised desire that burned in his eyes. The closest I'd come was when he'd joined Jazriel and me on the bed for a nap. I'd been hoping for a repeat of our first night together, but Jazriel seemed to be waiting for August to make the first move, and in the end, I'd fallen asleep.

I finally managed to call Ryls. After assuring her I was safe and everything was going fine, she immediately focused on another topic.

"Sooo… did you and August do it?" She giggled like we were teenagers at risk of being caught by our mothers.

Which was ridiculous. I didn't even have a mother.

"No. Wait! What do you know about August?" I demanded, glancing over my shoulder and half expecting to see him standing on the balcony and eavesdropping again.

"I know the world's grumpiest catbird is following you around like you're the cat's meow." Her playful banter sent a pang through me and I realized I missed her.

"Between us, August doesn't want to be mates."

Loud boos and foot stomping came through the phone.

"Um, yeah. The guys are here. But don't worry, they won't tell anyone." She must have covered the phone's speaker, because the next thing she said was muffled. "Because if you do, I swear y'all will be jerkin' your own gherkins for a month!"

"What does jerking your gherkin mean?" I asked, then twisted around to check on Jazriel, who made a sound like he'd inhaled a sneeze.

"You know! Hand to gland combat? Bopping the boloney? Holding the sausage hostage? Lubing the tube? Playing one-handed baseball? Playing tug of war with the cyclops? Pole dancing? Roughing up the suspect? Shake and steak? Wax on, whack off? Blow your own horn?"

Roars of laughter drowned out the rest of what she was saying, and I turned to Jazriel, hoping he'd been listening to my thoughts and could tell me what she was talking about.

"You don't know?" he wheezed, his face turning a mottled shade of red.

"If I knew, I wouldn't be asking you," I hissed.

Jazriel burst into laughter.

"Who's with you?" Ryls asked, her side of the call going instantly quiet.

I smiled as I watched Jazriel wipe tears from his eyes and shake his head over the joke I hadn't understood.

"My mate," I answered softly.

"YOUR MATE? You have a mate?!" Ryls squealed, nearly breaking my eardrum. "Like did the deed and completed the claim kind of mate?"

"Yes." I felt like I was glowing from the happiness bubbling in my chest.

"And? Who is he? What is he? What's his name? Where'd you meet? How do you feel?" Ryls asked eagerly.

"He's a pegasus who was being held by a group of men who were ex-employees at one of the labs. They took off with him when the lab was destroyed so they could take the research in other directions."

"Hey, give that back!" Ryls yelped.

"In a minute." Xerxes must have taken the phone from her, because his voice came loud and clear through the phone. "Iolani, are you absolutely sure he's a pegasus?"

I snorted. "Well, since I've spent hours riding him, yes, I'm sure."

"That's my girl!" Ryls shouted in the background. "Save a human, ride a pegasus!"

I blushed, belatedly realizing I'd made a poor word choice.

Your word choice was perfect, Jazriel assured me.

"So you've seen his pegasus form?" Xerxes pressed.

I scowled at the phone. "Yes, I have, and I'm wearing his hoofprint mark."

There was silence on the phone, and for a moment, I thought I'd been disconnected.

"Iolani, what is his name?" Xerxes voice was low, urgent.

Jazriel materialized at my side and gently took the phone from my hand and clicked the speaker button. "Hello, Xerxes Drakon. You know who I am."

"Jazriel Jouvellac," Xerxes whispered.

"Yes. Iolani has told me of the kindness you've shown her on behalf of your mate. You have nothing to fear from me as long as my mate considers you a friend." Jazriel spoke in a laid-back drawl, but there was an undercurrent of a threat beneath it.

I knew August had shown fear of Jazriel and distrust of pegasus in general, but I definitely felt like I was missing something.

"That is appreciated." For the first time since I'd known him, Xerxes sounded unsure. "What is Iolani to you?"

"She's the beat of my heart." Jazriel's hand cupped my face. "And the best thing in my life."

"You love her?" Xerxes' disbelief was palpable even over the phone.

"Yes." Jazriel answered without hesitation. Then his trademark grin lit his face. "She proposed to me, so we're getting married."

A strangled sound came from the other side of the

phone, and Jazriel smirked. I tried to read his thoughts, but they were shielded.

"You know what she has to do, right? And who she is?" Xerxes prodded.

"Yes, and I will lend my power however I can." Jazriel's fingers brushed through my hair.

For a species that didn't like to be petted, it sure seemed like his love language was physical touch.

Xerxes sighed. "Is there anything I should know?"

"I'm back and I just want to be left alone. But you can spread this warning: if anyone harms my Iolani, everyone on Earth will feel my wrath. And believe me, I've spent the last few decades coming up with really unique ways of making that happen. I'm willing to let the past remain in the past, but all bets are off the moment anyone lays a finger on my mate."

"Understood. I will make sure everyone knows." Xerxes handed the phone back to Ryls.

"What have you gotten yourself into, Lani?" she whispered as though our paranormal mates listening in on our conversation wouldn't be able to hear her.

My answer was easy. "Happiness."

We talked for several more minutes about the names in the notebook and August's stubbornness. I thanked her for sending Thom with the suitcase.

"No problem. If you need anything else, let us know. And the moment you're ready for my help, I'll be there," she promised.

"Ryls, take care of yourself, and the baby birdcat you're

growing. If your mates don't spoil you, tell me, and I'll kick their butts for you," I teased.

"And I'll come along," Jazriel offered, his eyes glinting with dark mischief.

"Will do, Lani." Ryls laughed. "And thanks, Jazriel. Judging by my mates' pale faces, they are going to let me do whatever I want just to keep you away. No offense."

Jazriel leaned toward the phone. "I consider it a compliment, and I look forward to meeting the phoenix who brought my mate to this world. I am in your debt."

We finished our goodbyes, and I powered off the phone.

I moved to straddle his lap. Picking up his hand, I pressed my cheek against his palm. "Are you going to explain what that was about?"

"One day. I'm not adding to your stress." Jazriel gave me a tender smile. "Just know that I will never hurt you."

"I know you won't." Dropping his hand, I kissed his cheek, then his nose, before brushing my lips against his mouth. "And Xerxes?"

"Xerxes is a good man. Our history was something he inherited, not something he caused. You can stop worrying about Ryls."

"Why is he scared of you?" I asked, then moaned when his hands slid under the nightie to touch my bare skin.

"Because I'm dangerous." He carried me to the bed, lowering me to my back on the mattress, and moved his body over mine. "Just by being alive and free, I'm a threat."

"I'm selfish." He pressed his lips to the hollow at the base of my throat.

"I'm jealous." His lips moved to place a kiss between my breasts.

"I always keep my promises... and threats." He sucked my nipple through the sheer fabric.

My eyes were crossing, and I writhed beneath him.

"And there is only one being on this earth that could challenge me and win."

"Oh? Who?" I panted, torn between wanting to know more, but also wanting him to shut up and keep his magical mouth on my skin.

"You." His fingers slipped between my thighs without warning, and I jerked off the bed. "Anything you ask of me, I will do. I'll give you the stars if you ask it. Just keep me."

"Jazriel Jouvellac, you belong to me." Sinking my fingers into his hair, I made him look me in the eye. "And I never give up what is mine."

16

IOLANI

"Iolani, wake up! We have to do this now!" The urgency in Jazriel's voice sent terror through me, and I bolted upright.

"What's going on?" I found Jazriel's glowing eyes in the dark room.

"The solar flares came a day earlier than expected. They are strong, so we should do this now." His hand squeezed mine. "You're strong and can handle this."

"Let's go," I whispered, kicking my legs free of the blanket and moving to dress in jeans and a shirt.

As I slipped on my hiking boots, I noticed the door between my room and August's was ajar. I finished tying my boot laces and pushed the door open wider, searching for the gryphon. His bed hadn't been slept in, and the room was empty.

Pale moonlight streamed through the glass door, landing on a piece of paper on the bed.

Picking it up, I unfolded the single sheet and read.

Iolani,

I've left, and this time I won't be coming back.

It's unfair for me to keep disappearing and reappearing in your life. I see the hope in your eyes that I will stay. You are beauty and sunshine, gentle and fragile. All the things I am not, and if I stay, I will only hurt you.

Thank you for the time we spent together. These days have been the best of my life and I will treasure them.

I had nothing to offer you, so I was unworthy to be your mate, but please know I will be faithful to you until my dying breath.

The pegasus is crazy, but he will protect you. But maybe you two should live in a city, away from wildlife. It would be safer for you.

August

I crumpled the paper and tossed it on the bed, then thought better of it and smoothed the paper. This was a letter I would probably reread hundreds of times.

Tears leaked down my cheeks. He had truly left this time, and he'd done it without giving me a chance to say goodbye.

"Because he knew you could convince him to stay." Jazriel pulled me to my feet and hugged me.

I would have time to grieve this loss later, but it was time to focus on my job. Closing my eyes, I called on the magic that the first phoenix had used to create me—for the sole purpose of protecting those who relied on me and keeping Cucalas safe.

I'd never failed, and tonight would be no exception.

Wiping my eyes, I straightened my spine and drew my royalty around me.

"I'm ready. Let's go."

Opening the glass balcony door, we stepped outside and spread our wings. I needed to be away from prying eyes and distractions. With a nod, we took to the cool night sky.

I KNEELED on the damp forest floor in a small meadow. Towering trees circled us, and looking up, I could see a star-studded sky.

"How can I help you without getting in your way?" Jazriel asked.

I pulled off my shirt. "Put your hands on my shoulders. The skin-to-skin contact should make it easier for me to pull the energy I need."

Without questioning me, Jazriel rested his palms on my shoulders. "I'm going to start drawing energy from the flares. Are you ready?"

Taking a deep breath, I released it, along with all my doubts and tension. "I'm ready."

Clearing my thoughts, I buried my fingers in the dirt. I called my magic, letting it build in my chest, but not releasing it. My skin began to glow as my body struggled to hold on to the ball of energy.

With a shout, I released the magic. It spread out from me like ripples around a stone dropped in a pond. The veil wobbled dangerously, and my stomach clenched when I realized how close we were cutting it.

Once my magic connected with the veil between the world I ruled and the world I was currently in, I began pouring my magic into it. The veil soaked up the energy like a plant in a drought.

Digging deep, I continued to send magic surging into it. Fire spread across my skin as my temperature climbed and I blinked away the sweat burning my eyes.

I was giving my all, but it was a drop in the bucket of what I needed. It was time to accept my mate's help.

Finding our bond, I opened myself fully to him. Untamed energy blasted into me, ricochetting around inside my body and burning what it touched. The sudden shock of pain caused me to lose focus, and the veil began to wobble.

No, no, no!

I refused to lose the progress I'd made. Ignoring the searing pain, I focused on letting Jazriel's magic surge straight through me and into the veil. This worked, and the steady flow of powerful energy began weaving through the very fabric of the veil.

I was so thrilled I barely paid attention to the scent of smoke in my nose and the way my lungs struggled to inflate. Fire had never been a danger for me, but this level of pure solar energy was unlike any power I'd touched before.

A knife sliced across my arm, and I hissed in pain. A heartbeat later, it sliced my cheek, and then my bare stomach. Looking down, I stared in confusion at the trickle of blood dripping down my abdomen.

"Something is here. It bears the mark of your magic, but beneath that, it is pure malevolence," Jazriel whispered.

"Azurea," I said through clenched teeth, still trying to keep focused so the flow of magic wouldn't be disrupted. "I thought she might come, but I didn't think she would have found enough energy to launch a physical attack."

Azurea's invisible nails sliced into my thigh, and a moment later raked across my breasts. I could fight her, but that would mean losing focus on the veil and possibly undoing the work that had been done.

"I can't direct my power at her while funneling energy from the sun or I could destroy this entire state. What do you want me to do?" Jazriel asked, his voice strained.

"Focus on the energy and ignore her." Clenching my jaw to keep from crying out, I let the soulless phoenix continue to tear at my flesh.

I could heal myself later. It was more important that I fixed the veil.

Realizing her attack wasn't going to stop me from stabilizing the veil, Azurea switched tactics.

Jazriel jerked behind me, cursing from the pain of her ghost claws. The magic pouring through our bond flickered, then Jazriel's fingers gripped my shoulders tighter.

Growling at the effort, Jazriel sent a flood of energy washing through me and straight into the veil. Minute by minute, the veil grew stronger.

Wind began whipping around us, and growing in

strength until the tree at the edge of the meadow began to bend and shake. Sticks and pebbles pelted our bodies, but still we fed energy into the veil.

Azurea's screams of fury tore at my ears. We were winning, and she wasn't going to stop us. She redoubled her efforts, this time releasing all her rage on my mate.

I wasn't sure how things worked for me since I wasn't a typical phoenix, but she was probably hoping that by killing my mate, she could kill me too. Permanently.

Closing my eyes, I reached for every bit of power I possessed and sent a blast of solar energy into the veil, while simultaneously sending my fire to encircle every inch of Jazriel's body and wings. Blue flames burst into the sky, showering glowing blue embers around us. It spread across the meadow, turning the grass to ash, and racing up the tree trunks.

Azurea released an inhuman screech as she slammed into the shield. Over and over, she tried to get him, growing angrier with each attempt.

Then the wind ceased, and the meadow was unnaturally silent.

Jazriel dropped to his knees behind me, but kept his hands on my shoulders. I touched him with the magic guarding him and realized he was on the verge of collapse, but was too stubborn to tell me.

The woven tapestry strengthening the veil was nearing completion, but I needed more time. I was trying to figure out how to cut off the flow from Jazriel before he burned out, while protecting him and also finding the power to finish.

An eery laugh whispered in the wind, and I braced myself for her next attack. I wasn't prepared for the crack of gunfire and the bullet that pierced my shoulder.

"Ah!" I cried out, biting down on my tongue at the shock of white-hot agony.

"You aren't going to win!" I screamed to the phoenix who'd tossed my mercies back into my face.

I felt the bullet pierce my chest before I heard the gunshot. Jazriel's wings wrapped around me, and his head dropped against my shoulder.

His heart beat was erratic, and win or lose, it was time to end this.

I touched Jazriel's skin and whispered in his mind, *Sleep, love.*

He was too weak to fight the telepathic command, and his muscles went limp. The solar power ceased as though a switch had been flipped, but I was ready.

Latching onto the living magic in my chest, I began to drain it into the veil, not giving it a chance to waver. If I was lucky, the veil would stabilize before I drained my very soul.

My vision blurred, and a wave of dizziness caused nausea to churn in my stomach. I bit down on my tongue, using the pain to keep me alert. Gunfire cracked, and a bullet whistled by my head.

Blood pounded in my ears as my rage grew. Wasn't it enough that I had to deal with a crazy soulless phoenix and a veil that could implode and take out a world or two? Why did I have to deal with a sniper, too?

Where had he come from, anyway? Had one of the men holding Jazriel escaped and followed us here?

My heart stuttered as I continued to push my magic into the veil, and the blue fire around me flickered to its unsteady beat. A visual representation of my internal fire going out.

I just hoped I'd have enough magic to revive. Otherwise, it would fall to Amaryllis to destroy Azurea once and for all.

My fire flickered, and the flames dimmed. Taking a deep breath, I prepared to risk it all.

Only to have a man drop to the ground beside me.

"August?"

17

IOLANI

A tiny bird made of blue flames hopped on his shoulder. It was the same bird I'd seen when I'd claimed Jazriel.

The little bird spread its wings and flew into my chest, disappearing in a shower of sparks. My waning magic flickered to life, weak but there.

"What do you need from me?" August pulled me into his arms.

"Protect Jazriel until he recovers," I whispered, closing my eyes to focus on sending the trickle of energy into the veil, fearing if I stopped, all my work would collapse around my feet. For all I knew, it was like those knitting projects where a single stitch that wasn't tied off could unravel the whole thing.

"There's a sniper shooting at us. So get the two of you out of here and somewhere safe."

"The pegasus can take care of himself," August snapped, pressing down on the gunshot wound in my side to stop the bleeding. "And I took out the shooter on my way in. It's going to be a challenge to ID what's left of him."

"He gave me too much energy. It's going to take a long time for him to recover."

"How did he do that? That's what you need, right? Magic?" August demanded, his fear making him harsh.

"You can't—"

"Jazriel said you recharge with food, sleep, and sex."

"It's claiming the mate bond that makes me stronger and causes my power to grow." My words slurred as I tried to answer him, but pushed the veil. "It's not just sex."

August pulled me into his lap, bracing my limp body against him. "Then claim me."

I shook my head. There was no way I would trap him as my mate after he'd made it clear it wasn't what he wanted.

"I want you, Iolani. You're mine and I'm never leaving your side again, whether you choose to claim me or not." August's lips captured my mouth.

It was a kiss full of passion and longing, and my waning magic leaped along the thread between us. Power arched between us as our souls swirled like birds in the air.

"Take it all. Take everything you need. Drain me, but don't use any more of your magic," August growled against my lips.

His shifter magic hit me like a tidal wave, and the trickle of magic I was feeding into the veil turned into a rushing river.

The demonic sounding screeches filled the air as Azurea

threw a tantrum. Her claws raked my back and down my neck.

August slowly lowered me onto the ground as he continued to kiss me, pouring his power and love into the bond. Then he covered me with his body and wrapped his wings around the three of us.

My ears popped with a pressure change as the veil snapped into place, steady and strong, with our magic weaving through it.

"Is it done?" August asked.

"Yes. We did it," I whispered.

"Then sleep." August's lips pressed against my forehead. "I'll protect you both for the rest of our lives."

I wanted to tell him that was going to be a very long time, but sleep claimed me.

"Well, you definitely aren't an early bird." A feminine voice drifted into my dreams. "I need you to open your eyes. We are running out of time, and I need to tell you something before I have to go take care of things."

With no small amount of effort, I squinted in the direction the voice was coming from. "Did I die?"

She laughed. "Close, but no cigar."

Propping myself up on my elbow, I blinked at the woman with pale hair and brilliant blue eyes who watched me. "Belle?"

She held up her hands in surrender. "Guilty as charged."

I rubbed my head. This had to be a dream.

"It's a vision—just like the other two I showed you." Belle pulled a nail file out of the thin air and filed her nail.

"That was you?" I asked, stunned. "I thought it was Azurea."

"You think she would be helpful?" Belle scoffed. "No, we are on a tight timeline and I need you mated and at full power—like, yesterday."

"I don't even know you, so there is no way we're working on anything together." Lying back down, I closed my eyes and waited for the dream to change.

Belle chuckled. "You can't get rid of me that way. But I do have somewhere to be, so listen up, buttercup."

"Fine. Let's do this." Opening my eyes, I motioned for her to start talking.

"There is a gemstone store in Colorado where you need to be this coming weekend. It has to be this weekend. Capeesh?"

"In case you didn't know, I drained my energy to non-existent levels. It will take me weeks to recover." I laughed bitterly, frustrated that I'd gained my strength back only to have it yanked away two days later.

"Wrong. You need to finish marking the gryphon. That man has been a thorn in my side with all his talon dragging, but he has a lot of bottled-up passion and he's close to erupting. That's going to do amazing things for your magic reserves."

She disappeared and reappeared a second later on the edge of the bed beside me. "And your paranormal black beauty is going to wake up more powerful than he's been in centuries."

"How could you possibly know that?" I narrowed my eyes, scrutinizing her face for signs of deception.

Belle shrugged. "I'm a Watcher. It's my job to know stuff."

"So why will he be stronger?" I asked.

"Something to do with old curses, an assassination attempt gone wrong, and dragon blood..." She waved her hand dismissively.

"He'll explain all that at some point. The long and short of it is your fire has been burning through him since you healed him and again when you claimed each other. That fire has been burning through his body and cleansing it. Last night, you pretty much turned him into a tiki torch, and literally sweat lodged what was left of the dark magic that was binding the bulk of his power."

My jaw dropped. "The *bulk* of it? You mean he's not been at full strength?"

She grinned. "Honey, you are so good with phoenixes, but have so much to learn about other species. That man has practically been walking around with both his hands metaphorically tied behind his back."

No wonder Xerxes had sounded scared.

"Now you just need to go get your third mate. He's going to seem a bit boring compared to August and Jazriel, but give him time. And you aren't going to feel the bond in the same way you do with shifters."

"How will I know where to go or who he is?" I asked, my mind spinning with all the information she was dumping on me.

"I've left the directions on a sheet of paper in your back-pack. And his name is Orland Claiborne."

"I have to deal with Azurea. Going on a trip to a rock shop isn't really something I have time for."

Belle chewed her lip. "Listen, I can't tell you more than I already have. But I need you to trust me. You need to make this your top priority."

She could have been steering me wrong, but I didn't think so. It was because of her that I'd been where I needed to be to find Jazriel. I might be an idiot, but I was going to trust her.

I wasn't sure what the guys would think, but I nodded my agreement. "Okay. I'll find a way to get to the rock store by this weekend."

A brilliant smile lit up her face. "Good! You won't regret it."

"I've got to get moving, but I'll see you again soon." She hopped to her feet and stretched. "Two last things. Remember that not everything is as it seems, so trust your instincts. And next time you talk to Amaryllis, tell her Arabelle says hi."

"You've met Ryls?" I sat up.

Belle, or Arabelle, twisted her lips in a wry smile. "Once.

I was checking in on her, but ended up in a tight spot. She helped me out."

Before I could pry for more information, she wiggled her fingers, and the vision went dark.

18

AUGUST

I paced the bedroom, staring at the motionless bodies of my mate and the man I envied more than any other being on earth because she loved him.

There was something different about the Jazriel I'd known yesterday and the one currently sleeping like a baby. He'd always been powerful, but even in his sleep, alpha energy rolled off him with each rise and fall of his chest.

I shouldn't have been affected by it, but I was. Although I'd never admit it to the arrogant stallion.

Iolani's eyelids fluttered, drawing me from my inner musings. Sitting down on the bed beside her, I brushed my knuckles across her cheek.

"Bluebird?" I whispered, desperate for her to wake, but also wanting her to sleep as long as she needed.

"Hm?" she asked, her voice husky. Then her big blue eyes opened. "August?"

"I'm here."

"How long was I asleep?" she asked, pressing her fingertips to her eyes.

"Almost twenty-four hours." I stared at the bandages covering her body and rage boiled up inside me.

"And Jazriel?" she whispered, trying to push herself into a sitting position.

"He's beside you." I gently pushed her back down on the pillow. "As far as I can tell, he is uninjured, but he's a ridiculously heavy sleeper. I dropped him once, and he slept through it."

Her eyes widened. "Because I ordered him to. He's not going to wake until I undo it."

I gaped at her. "What if you had died?"

"If I'd died, the command would have been released. I think."

I was never going to get on her bad side. The last thing I wanted was for her to turn me into Rip Van Wynkle. "So now what? You wake sleeping beauty with true love's kiss?"

Iolani rolled her eyes, then reached out a hand to stroke his hair. "Time to wake up, Jazriel."

He was lying on the bed one moment, and the next, he'd pulled the blanket off her and was running his hands over her body. "My love, you must be in so much pain."

"I'm too relieved to be in pain," she lied. "I'm here with you two and the veil is stable. Nothing else matters right now."

Smoke drifted from his hands and swirled up his forearms to his elbows. "Be still and let me care for you."

Taking his time, he removed the bandages and healed the wounds one by one. When he finished, there wasn't a speck of blood or a mark on her skin.

"That's new," she whispered, her eyes huge as she looked up at him. "Arabelle wasn't kidding."

Jazriel tilted his head. "Arabelle?"

"I mean Belle. Remember her from the lounge chairs?"

"But what does she have to do with this?" Jazriel asked.

I listened silently as Iolani babbled on about everything in her vision, feeling my heart sink the longer she talked.

Jazriel clearly understood what she was talking about, which showed me how close they'd become. She'd confided so much in him.

I wanted her to trust me enough to tell me when she needed me, just as she'd let Jazriel follow her into that hellscape of a battle the previous night. There were so many things I wanted to ask her, but I remained silent.

"What do you want to know first?" Iolani asked, locking her eyes on me.

"You can read thoughts?"

She nodded. "It hasn't worked the same on Earth as it did on Cucalas."

"I can read thoughts too," Jazriel volunteered as if this was a sharing circle.

"Yeah, I know," I growled.

"Really? How'd you figure it out?"

I snorted. "When you started insulting me in my head."

Jazriel nodded. "Yeah, that was a risk."

I turned my attention back to Iolani. "Cucalas?"

"My world, the phoenix afterlife." She crawled across the bed, climbing onto my lap, facing me. "I'm a phoenix, and I was blasted through the veil between our worlds when I helped Ryls return to her mates."

"You're a phoenix." All the pieces of the puzzle that didn't make sense fell into place. "You didn't survive the crash landing on that cliff. Or the waterfall. Or the horse running away with you. Or Jazriel throwing you off his back. You died all those times, didn't you?"

She nodded, not meeting my eyes.

"Hey! She forced me to throw her, so I didn't kill her." Jazriel scowled at her.

"I still owe you for that one," she said.

It made so much sense, and I wanted to bang my head against a wall for not putting it together sooner. The missing clothes, the lack of fear when facing death, the insanely fast healing, the flashes of blue I sometimes caught from the corner of my eye that must have been her fire.

I finally swallowed back my bitterness and looked at the intricate mark that Iolani had left on Jazriel's chest.

The night they'd completed the bond, her sweet arousal had scented the forest, drawing me to her like a fly to honey.

Jazriel had spotted me almost instantly and had angled their bodies so I wouldn't miss seeing him touch what could have been mine. I'd left before they'd marked each other, so I hadn't been able to bring myself to look at the mark fully before that moment.

It was a phoenix. I'd purposely avoided looking too

closely at any of the signs that pointed to her identity because I knew it would only make it harder to walk away.

It's about freaking time, Jazriel yelled in my mind, the corner of his mouth twitching as he caught my wince.

Ignoring his attempt to aggravate me, I wondered if his actions had a deeper motive than simple gloating or male possessiveness. If he wanted her for himself, why did he continue trying to taunt me into getting over my insecurities and show her how I felt?

From the rumors about pegasus, they weren't the type to share anything, especially not a bed. Yet Jazriel had left a space for me to sleep beside Iolani wherever we camped.

Even in that moment of sacred intimacy where they came together as mates, he hadn't tried to hide her beautiful body from me or exclude me. No, he'd let me watch the emotions and pleasure on her face.

Jazriel snorted, then spoke into my mind. *Yeah, to please my mate. I tried to get you to give in to what I knew both of you wanted. But don't get it twisted… I attempted to push past my selfish desire to have Iolani to myself, but I seriously enjoyed rubbing it in your face.*

Okay, he was definitely still a jackass.

Pegasus, Jazriel corrected. *And for the record, our mate gets really turned on when you're involved. Even if you just stand there motionless while I do all the work.*

Not sure what to say to that, I turned back to Iolani. "Why didn't you tell me what you needed from me? I never would have left. Last night, I could've given you power before you got hurt."

I struggled to keep my voice from shaking. "Instead, I'm camping not too far from the lodge because I can't bear to take another step away from you, and a fiery blue bird shows up. I was so sure I was conjuring it in my mind, until it landed on my shoulder and electrified the crap out of me until I got up. And every time I stopped following it, the tiny sadist would swoop back and light me up again."

Jazriel snickered. "I would give half my fortune to see that."

"You think it's funny? Look at my back!" I sat Iolani on the bed and lifted my shirt to show him.

Jazriel's laughter boomed in the small room. "I got a blue mane that matches Iolani's hair and an intricate tattoo, and you look like you fought a grill and lost."

"August!" Iolani sobbed, moving to her knees on the bed so she was level with my back. "My magic did all of this?"

"Of course not. Most of it is from whatever was attacking you two when I arrived." I tried to pull my shirt down, but she wouldn't let me.

Jazriel's laughter faded, and Iolani's fingers traced the deep gashes that criss-crossed my back and shoulders. In some places, I'd been scratched in the same place so many times that glimpses of my ribs could be seen.

While I'd waited for them to wake up, those had stitched themselves together, so at least she didn't have to see the full extent of the attack.

"I thought she stopped attacking us because she'd used up her energy and faded to the point that she couldn't physically touch the living without another recharge. But she didn't leave. You let her attack you instead." Iolani's fingers grew hot against my skin, and I quickly turned, catching both her hands in one of mine.

"Don't you dare try to heal me," I growled. "I will heal with time, and you need to save your energy and rest."

"But that has to hurt!" She tried to pull her hands free, but I refused to let go, needing her to know I wasn't going to back down on this.

Jazriel sighed and pushed to his feet. "Allow me." Smoke curled around his fingers and circled my skin.

"I would've healed," I pointed out, uncomfortable accepting his help, even if I did appreciate the pain disappearing.

Jazriel shrugged. "Yeah, you would. But it's upsetting our mate. She wants you to look pretty, since you're far more delicate than her."

His eyes glinted with anger, then he blinked and it was gone. "You have a lot to learn about our mate. So let's start with this: make her cry again, and I won't be anywhere near as understanding and patient as I've been thus far."

Dropping his hand from my shoulder, he sat back down on the bed, this time beside Iolani.

As I stared into her big blue eyes, the memory of seeing her in the middle of the scorched earth with bullet holes in her skin, still trying to protect Jazriel's fallen body as the wind screamed and an unseen monster lacerated her skin, was a sight I'd relive in my nightmares for centuries to come.

She'd refused to give up, even as I'd listened to the slowing of her heartbeat.

"Why didn't you trust me enough to tell me?" I dropped to my knees in front of her. "I never would have left your side."

Iolani brushed her fingers through my hair. "It wasn't about trust, August. I knew you would be willing to face any monster for me, because you'd consider it your duty.

"But I didn't want you to be with me out of some misguided notion of honor and obligation. I wanted you to be there because you wanted me," she whispered, brushing her fingers along my stubbled jaw.

Iolani thinks you claimed her because the pull of the mate bond forced you to, Jazriel spoke in my mind. *Now set the freaking record straight so she can be happy and you two can finish claiming each other.*

"Iolani, I resisted the pull of the mate bond. It was uncomfortable and mildly irritating, but I could have kept resisting it. A bond is a sign of a good match, and it encourages our beasts to mate and mark. Have I been rock hard every day since I saw you on Xerxes' lawn? Yes. I'm wildly attracted to you, and you are the first woman to cause me to experience lust. But I could resist that."

Her lips were parted, and she barely breathed as she listened.

"It was you I couldn't resist. It was your laughter I woke up wanting to hear. It was the joy you find in everything around you and the kindness you show to both humans and animals. It was the adventure of hours spent trail riding with you, never knowing what waited for us around the next bend.

"It was falling asleep with you next to me, and waking to find you covering me with your wing because you wanted me to be comfortable. I fell more in love with you every single day. I want to make love to you until you can't walk straight and Jazriel would have to carry you every-where. But that's not because of the pull of the bond, and it's not why I begged for you to accept me as your mate last night."

"It's not?" Iolani asked.

"No, it's because I can't imagine a single day of my life that doesn't have you in it. I want your heart."

"August." Tears streamed down her face.

"I'm asking again. Iolani, will you claim me and mark me as yours?"

Her answer was to throw herself into my arms, toppling us backward onto the floor.

19

IOLANI

August held me against his chest, laughing softly. He'd dropped the walls he used to hide behind, and instead of looking away, he held eye contact. My heart melted as he let me see everything he felt for me.

After our partial bond last night, I'd been able to pick up part of his thoughts and finally understood why he'd been so determined to leave. This man, who thought he couldn't show me love, had so much love in his eyes it stole my breath.

Last night, he'd protected not only my body, but Jazriel's because it mattered to me. Not once had he winced, groaned, or shown any sign of the damage being done to his back. He'd kissed me like we were the only two there, and all the while he'd been taking the blows meant for me.

Then he'd managed to get the three of us back to the lodge and guarded us all day, ignoring his need to rest and heal.

For a man who didn't think he could love me enough,

he'd shown a depth of devotion and love beyond my wildest dreams.

August cupped my face, his touch slightly hesitant. Was that because he worried I was weak and needed to rest? Or was he afraid of moving too fast and pushing me away?

"So what's next, my beautiful bluebird?" His hand was so large it covered half my face, and he easily brushed his thumb across my bottom lip. "I want to make sure I'm part of the team, and that I'm there when you need me."

"You were there when I needed you. Just like you were when the cliff collapsed, and when the bear tried to eat me, and when the moose tap-danced on me." Darting out my tongue, I licked his thumb, enjoying the flare of his nostrils and the rumble in his chest that such a simple touch caused.

He'd gone from feeling nothing to feeling everything.

"I was going to figure out how to capture Azurea, or at least how to lure her back into Cucalas. But Arabelle says I need to go to Colorado first." This time, when August's thumb brushed my bottom lip, I sucked it into my mouth.

"Iolani," he groaned, and his length twitched where it was pressed between our bodies.

"Do you trust her?" Jazriel asked, sliding from the bed to the floor beside us.

Releasing August's thumb with a pop, I nodded. "I do. She helped me find you."

"And what are you supposed to find there?" Jazriel's eyes glittered in anticipation... but of what?

I scrunched my nose, trying to figure out what mischief he was up to. His mind was quiet, not giving me any clues.

"Orland Claiborne," I answered warily. "My third mate—"

August snarled, his right hand sliding to my throat. "You should have worn my mark first, and it's my fault that didn't happen. But I swear I will not allow another male to have your body before me."

"Oh," I squeaked, shocked at his shift from labrador to feral wolf.

Yessss! Jazriel hissed. *Get ready, because he's about to erupt from the sexual tension he's been building up.*

Jazriel had known how August would react to the mention of another male, and was practically rubbing his hands together in glee.

His left hand gripped my butt, grinding his hips upward against me. "You are mine, Iolani of Cucalas."

I should probably tell him I'm the Queen of Cucalas...

Definitely not! Jazriel protested. *Let's save that for another day. Now, brace yourself...*

What are you planning?

Jazriel winked at me. "August, I may have taken her first, but I kept myself from tasting her... barely."

August's body vibrated beneath me. "Is this true? He hasn't devoured you?"

"He hasn't." My cheeks burned and my body warmed as I imagined his tongue lapping at the ache between my thighs.

Jazriel pulled me off August and settled me on the floor between his powerful thighs. He pressed my back against his chest, then gently parted my legs, opening me to

August's hungry gaze.

"You seem to have a particular fixation on tasting her, so I've waited to show her this particular pleasure. Consider us even for saving my life the night we first met."

August was kneeling between my thighs before Jazriel stopped speaking. When he leaned in, my thighs trembled, and on reflex, I started to close my thighs.

Jazriel held my thighs open, giving August access to my soaked heat. It was insanely erotic to have my mate offering me up to my other mate.

August's head dipped, and he breathed the fragrance of my arousal deep into his lungs. My pulse pounded in my ears and my body flushed again.

When August lay flat on his belly and pressed a soft kiss to my throbbing entrance, I nearly wept.

"So sweet," he purred, his tongue tracing the length of my slit.

"August," I moaned, wanting more but finding it dirty to tell him what I needed.

"She wants you to be rough," Jazriel volunteered.

"Jaz— OH!" I whimpered as August's tongue plunged deep inside my tight channel.

The now familiar building of pleasure in my stomach wound itself tighter with each lap of his tongue. When he ground his tongue against my clit, I gasped, arching off the floor.

August laughed, his mouth pressed tight against me and sending vibrations through my over sensitive nerves. He alternated lapping up my arousal and delving his tongue inside me. The dark need inside me demanded release, but still he continued to bring me to the edge and then back away right before pleasure erupted.

Jazriel's hands moved to cup my breasts, kneading the aching flesh and sending more slick heat between my thighs. August purred in delight, and his hands slipped under my butt, tilting my pelvis to give him better access. This time, when his tongue plunged inside me, it was thicker, stretching me as it licked at the cream far deeper than a human tongue could reach.

My fingers sank into his hair, shamelessly holding him between my thighs as I writhed between my mates. The men worked my body into a frenzy, refusing to allow me my release until I was begging.

With a final thrust of his tongue, I shattered into a thousand pieces—or at least that's what it felt like. I rode the waves of pleasure, screaming as August caused a second and third orgasm thanks to his eagerness to lap up the rush of cream that accompanied my orgasms.

"So beautiful." Jazriel's voice was husky as he stared down into my eyes.

August pulled back, placing a final soft kiss on my inner thigh. His eyes were heavy-lidded, and he licked his lips. He stood, shoving his pants over his hips and letting his erection spring free. I watched, utterly mesmerized, as he gripped it, running his hand along the length.

"Feed him," August ordered.

"Wh…what?" I croaked. This was not the time to stop for food.

"Dip your fingers into your cream and let him taste you."

I trembled with lust, thoroughly turned on by his dominance. But what if Jazriel doesn't want it…

"I want it." Jazriel's breathing had turned harsh. "You have no idea."

My hand shook as I dipped my fingers inside and felt them grow slick.

"Good girl." August's voice was pure gravel and his hand movements grew rougher on his erection.

Tilting my head back, I offered the two fingers to Jazriel. He sucked them into his mouth, humming in pleasure as his tongue circled my fingers to get every drop.

My temperature soared and fire flickered on my skin, "I… I… need—"

I didn't have to finish asking for what I wanted. Without a word of discussion, and in a single smooth movement, the men flipped me around and put me on my knees, facing Jazriel.

August gripped my hip with his left hand and used his right to guide his hard erection inside me. Once he'd pushed in as far as he could go, August moved both hands to my hips. With each roll of his hips, August rocked my hips in perfect rhythm.

All I could do was try to breathe as he stoked that feral lust pacing in my belly. As he thrust into me faster, and his movements turned rougher, I placed a hand on Jazriel's shoulder to steady myself.

He ducked his head and sucked my nipple into the heat of his mouth.

"Ooooh. I don't think I can handle this," I gasped.

Instead of slowing, August plunged harder into me and Jazriel's mouth licked and sucked with enthusiasm.

Using my free hand, I reached down and wrapped my fingers along Jazriel's stiff erection. My pegasus mate groaned, his hot breath against my skin.

Loving his sensitivity to my touch, I called my magic to my hand and carefully sent tiny electrical pulses into his cock.

Jazriel cursed and thrust himself into my hand. "You are playing dirty, little mate. But two can play at this game."

His fingers brushed against my ribs, and my breasts, and my neck, and my legs... all at the same time. But that was impossible.

Blinking through my lust, I glanced down to find wisps of dark smoke rolling from his hands. They teased and stroked, touch me everywhere. It was a sensation overload.

"I'm so close," I panted. "Please."

August shifted slightly, and when he thrust inside me again, it stroked me in all the right ways. At the same time, Jazriel's wispy magic teased my clit and his tongue curled around the hardened peak of my nipple.

I came, screaming their names as stars exploded in my vision. I'm pretty sure I was seeing the Milky Way galaxy as I tried to keep from passing out from the pure ecstasy of making love with both my mates.

My walls clamped around August, milking him.

"You're mine!" he roared as orgasmic pleasure rocked him.

"Yes, yours," I whimpered.

Fiery magic burst from my chest and circled our heads. From the corner of my eye, I watched it drop behind August. My heart swelled as my mark was branded on his back.

August wrapped his fingers around my upper arm, and his hand began to glow. When he pulled away, I stared in awe at the talons wrapped around my bicep.

When my lust had exploded and my magic had burst free, I'd accidentally sent a surge straight into Jazriel's erection. He'd shouted in pleasure, and his cock jerked in my hand as he joined us in bliss.

We collapsed onto the floor, my sweat-slick body tangling with my mates'. It was ten minutes before any of us found the strength to speak.

I broke the silence. "So how long before we can do that again?"

"You have no idea how much I want to, but we're going to need some time to recover." August's words were muffled against my lower back. "I'm not sure I will ever be able to move again."

"I think I might have pulled every muscle in my body," Jazriel groaned. "For a minute there, I thought I was going to die."

"But you didn't die." I laughed, licking Jazriel's chest, and lacing my fingers with August's. "So just walk it off!"

ABOUT SEDONA ASHE

Sedona Ashe doesn't reserve her sarcasm for her books; her poor husband can tell you that her wit, humor, and snarky attitude are just part of her daily life. While she loves writing paranormal shifter reverse harem novels, she's a sucker for true love, twisted situations, and wacky humor.

Sedona lives in a small town at the base of the Great Smoky Mountains in Tennessee. She and her husband share their home with their three children, adorable pup, five cats, two pet foxes, chickens, three crazy turkeys, two cows, and over a hundred reptiles.

When she isn't working, she enjoys getting away from the computer to hike, free dive, travel, study languages, and capture the essence of places and people in her photography. She has a crazy goal of writing one million words in a year and spending six months exploring Indonesia.

www.ingramcontent.com/pod-product-compliance
Lightning Source LLC
Chambersburg PA
CBHW020435180626
46812CB00003B/1248